Murderous CONsequences

A Sadie Sabatini Mystery
Book 1

Nicole Leiren

ISBN: 978-1-963705-10-2

Published in the United States of America by Harbor Lane Books, LLC.

www.harborlanebooks.com

This book is dedicated to the first person in the publishing world who took a chance on me, believed in me, and never gave up. To Dawn Dowdle, I thank you for your unwavering faith and your friendship. Thank you for helping Sadie's story have the chance to be told. I hope you're getting to do the most amazing puzzles in Heaven. You are missed!

Chapter One

What in God's name am I doing here?

Seriously?

I glanced around the room, my head on a swivel, and took in my surroundings. It was a Wednesday night—happy hour at The Club, as the locals called it. I found a great deal of amusement in the idea that discounted drinks and free appetizers for a couple hours were supposed to make people happy. There was so much more to life. I should know. I'd lived so many already.

The mahogany bar I sat at sipping my wine hinted at affluence and the stone fireplace, even though it wasn't lit, conveyed a sense of warmth throughout the room. Large wooden beams strategically placed along the ceiling led to a wall of windows that framed a breathtaking view of Lake Amore.

The lake. It was why I was here in Wilson, Texas. The love of everything Italian was in my DNA, thanks to my father and his heritage. Finding a lake that literally meant love in Italian had called to me with an irresistible siren song. The fact no one knew me here...well, in all truthfulness, was the primary reason I'd chosen it.

The bar was filling up fast. The muddled conversations drifted up to the rafters, transitioning to a comforting hum of humanity thrumming in and around the bar. It wouldn't take a rocket scientist for anyone entering the room to recognize I was the new stranger in town.

Wilson, Texas, sported a population of five hundred eighty-six–well, eighty-seven once I moved in. A weekend or retirement home for those who either had been born into money in a fancy birthing suite or made their money from "hard" work like oil and gas executives and financial geniuses. I knew the type. Rich people who pretended they were like everyone else, while inwardly looking down on the rest of society. I'd learned a lot over the years from hanging out with the stereotypes who called this place their home. And what I knew, I could control.

While I knew them, they didn't know me. And in a small town, that placed me in the center circle of Barnum & Bailey's circus of life. I'd garnered more than a few curious glances before the onlooker noticed a recognizable face or made their way to sit with friends. It was as bad as high school. Maybe worse. Men stared at my cleavage and women, my hair. I didn't blame them. I'd gone to a lot of effort to make sure both of those items were what people focused on. Not wanting to be identifiable by someone later had been an occupational hazard.

This was ridiculous. I didn't really want to get to know anyone apart from what I'd already learned from my pre-move research. I'd hoped to offer a smile or two, pass out a few cards, and invite people to the opening of my new shop, Tesoro. A girl had to make a living, right? Or at least pretend to.

Since this was the worst idea I'd had well...ever, I downed the rest of my pinot noir and placed a twenty on the bar to cover my "happy" hour drink and a generous tip. Just as I slid off my bar stool, a woman several inches shorter than me with a cherub face and auburn curls piled high on her head came up to me, smiled, and extended her hand. If I had to guess her age, I would place my bet on the mid-forties, but with the miracles of modern makeup and treatments, it was also possible my guess was skewed. "You must be new here. I'm Kelsey and this..." she gestured to a man who was thick in the middle and missing some hair on top, "...is my husband, Pete."

Wanting to make my escape, I shook her hand. 'I'm Sadie Sabatini. And if by new you mean less than three weeks in town, then guilty as charged."

She laughed. I guessed what I said could be taken as a joke. Sadly, unless I was running a con where I clearly knew the objective of my interaction with others, I struggled a bit at so-called normal conversation. "Well, we've not seen you here at the club, have we, Pete?"

Pete's gaze traveled up and down my five-foot ten-inch frame before stopping for just a moment longer than necessary at my cleavage, then resumed the journey to my face. His grin lent itself more to a leer, but I ignored that. "No, and I'd remember seeing her."

Kelsey playfully pushed him. "Behave!" She gestured to a table with another couple seated next to the window. "Please join us for a drink and tell us what brought you to Wilson."

While I really did want to make my escape, part of my new objective was blending in and finding that new *normal*. As a result, I returned her warm smile. "Let me grab a fresh glass of wine, and I'll join you in a few moments."

"Wonderful!" Kelsey offered with enthusiasm. "I love introducing people and strengthening the bonds of small-town Texas."

Drawing a deep breath, I returned her smile. "That's why I'm here. To become part of the fabric of small-town..." I almost said USA, but remembered the pride each Texan has in their state. The flag boasting the red, white, and blue with the single star flew proudly on buildings, homes, and streets everywhere in the state. I was impressed, to be honest. "Texas. It's a beautiful state, and Wilson and Lake Amore are wonderful."

"Smart and beautiful," Kelsey bragged. "You're going to do well here."

From her lips to God's ears. I needed this to go well. After a lifetime of being on the move, and sometimes, the run, I wanted to find a nice, quiet place to settle down and just be...well, me. "Thanks, Kelsey. I appreciate your kindness."

A few minutes later, I found myself being introduced to several other people as everyone stopped by to say hello to Kelsey and Pete. Though my initial reaction to Pete was less than positive, maybe I just needed to get to know him a little better. I'd reserve judgment for now.

I was just starting to get comfortable and relax when I noticed out of the corner of my eye a man being denied the opportunity to sit at a long table of people who were giving off a we're-better-than-everyone-else vibe. That simple act sparked a chain reaction in my nervous system that ended with the short hairs on the back of my neck standing at attention. I'd always had a thing for the underdog. In fact, it started in high school when I devoted significant time to creatively finding ways to even the playing field for those whom society had deemed less important. I hadn't stood for it as a teenager, and I sure wasn't going to stand for it now. I returned my attention to Kelsey and leaned closer to her. "Thank you for your kindness this evening. I truly appreciate it and hope we can get to know each other better in the coming days." Using my gaze to draw her attention over to the man I'd spotted, "If you'll excuse me, I think I see someone who might need a kind gesture as well."

Her gaze followed mine to see the someone I'd referenced. After a moment, her expression softened and she nodded. "Of course. Please tell Jonathan I said hello."

"I will. Thank you again." I started to get up to head to the bar for another drink. Her touch on my arm stopped my progress. "He likes Jack Daniel's, just in case you'd like to buy him a drink to cheer him up."

Something about Kelsey's manner told me she was one of the good gals. I pulled a few cards from my purse and handed them to her. "Thank you again for your kindness tonight. I'd love it if you stopped by the grand opening of my shop tomorrow. All the information is on here."

She took the cards. "We'll try."

A moment later, I'd secured another wine and a Jack Daniel's and made my way to the table where Jonathan was seated, by himself, eating some of the free appetizers. For the record, he looked anything but happy. He was small in stature but had held his head high, even when he was being shunned. I liked that kind of fight in a person. He wasn't handsome by classic standards, but the salt-and-pepper hair, mostly still pepper, gave way to a strong jaw and tanned skin that some women might like. He was probably older than he looked, but the number in my head placed him close to fifty, maybe.

"Hi. Is this seat taken?" I offered my best smile as I held out the glass of whiskey.

The look on his face was priceless. I gave him ten extra bonus points for his gaze immediately going to my face. He stood and came to the other side of the table to pull out a chair for me. "Only by the most beautiful woman in Wilson. Please, sit down."

We sipped our drinks in silence for a few moments before he set his glass down. "Do I know you?"

I shook my head. "I'm new in town. I don't think anyone *knows* me yet." I handed him a card. "You're welcome to come to the grand opening of my new store tomorrow, though."

He laughed, tucking the card in the breast pocket of his shirt without even looking at it. "My apologies. I pride myself on never forgetting a face. But you're right, if I'd seen you before, I certainly wouldn't forget. You can rejoin your friends, Miss...?"

I was pretty good with faces, too, so I was certain I didn't know Jonathan and it didn't appear he knew me. Otherwise, all my efforts to find a place to lay low for a while would have been in vain. I also prided myself on paying attention to my surroundings. During our conversation, I observed that, even though the chatter at the table Jonathan hadn't been allowed to sit at had continued, their gazes kept finding their way back to us. I decided it would be fun to give them a show. I took his hand and smiled. "Sabatini. Sadie Sabatini. Besides Kelsey, whom I met right before you and made it her personal mission to introduce me to everyone, you're the only friend I have here in the community."

This man's smile melted a little of the tough exterior I'd donned to help me survive all the years that preceded my arrival here. "Well, you're one of the few I've had since I moved here six months ago."

My heart wilted at his statement. I thought small-town communities were supposed to be more welcoming than the big city. Maybe there was a probationary period before you found your *in*. Either way, I wasn't going to let tonight be sad and lonely for Jonathan. While staying under the radar was my original goal, sometimes one had to adjust to do what seems right. "You wanna get out of here and go on a boat ride?"

"Heck yeah, I do. You got a boat?" He stood, offering his hand.

"I do." I smiled and took it, enjoying every curious glance directed at our little center of attention. The spotlight was certainly on the middle ring now. Score was now one for the underdog and a big zilch for the pretentious people who only wanted to hang with their own kind.

We sashayed past the table of people who'd shunned him, and I gave my long, coal black hair a nice toss as I slipped my arm around Jonathan's shoulders. Not wanting to completely alienate the people at the long table—one never knew what connection might come in handy in the future, I stopped at the head of the table and made sure I had everyone's attention. "Good evening. I don't think I've had the pleasure of meeting any of you. I'm Sadie Sabatini, new proprietor in town." I reached in my purse with the hand not currently around Jonathan's shoulder and pulled out some cards. Laying them on the table, I added "I hope to see each of you in my shop this week. It's the grand opening and I'm offering a ten percent discount to the first ten patrons."

The woman sitting closest to me picked up the cards and started handing them down the table. "Nice meeting you, Ms. Sabatini."

Offering my brightest smile, I squeezed Jonathan's

shoulder. "Thank you. I look forward to getting to know each of you soon. Now, if you'll excuse Jonathan and me, we're heading out for a sunset boat ride."

Once outside, he was grinning ear to ear. "You like messing with people, don't you?"

"I like messing with people who think they're above being messed with."

He chuckled. "I like messing with them all."

I wasn't sure what he meant by that but figured I'd get him to tell me more another time. This evening we would fully enjoy Lake Amore as the sun started to set over the glassy water. I led him to my golf cart. "Your chariot awaits."

"Seriously?"

"I live in a golf cart community. While within the confines of said community, I intend to drive a golf cart. Now, do you want to go boating or not?"

Jonathan slid in next to me and a moment later we were heading down Marina Drive, which led to the community marina that housed my boat. The setting sun filtering through the trees supplied a picturesque backdrop of shadow and light as we made our way slowly along the short distance to the marina. Townhomes with a lake view lined the left side of the road while dog parks and playgrounds occupied the right. Though most of Wilson was made up of retired people or those who didn't have to work, grandchildren often came for visits, so it was important to the community for them to have a nice place to play.

"What brought you to Wilson?" Out of habit, I decided to start building a mental file on Jonathan with a little background information. I'd learned over the years it helped to understand what motivated people by knowing where they came from.

His thin frame turned toward me, and the reflection off

his dark-rimmed glasses made it hard to see his eyes. "Would you believe me if I told you revenge?"

Schooling my features to make sure they revealed nothing, I shrugged. "I have no reason not to believe you."

"Good answer," he chuckled.

"So, you lived here before?" I turned the golf cart into the parking lot of the marina, wishing there'd been a little more road between The Club and here.

He got out of the cart and walked around the front, took my hand, and helped me out. Though I obviously didn't need the assistance, I always appreciated a gentleman.

He kissed my hand and winked, "My mother lived here a lifetime ago. She left when she was pregnant with me."

"Is she here with you now to help with your plan of revenge?" My tone was light and teasing, but I really wanted to delve deeper into his earlier statement. Curiosity was equally good and bad at times.

We started over the bridge that led to the security gate to the boat slips. On the right was a snack shack of sorts that served boaters and families during prime time. On the left, the structure that housed management and staff, and just on the other side of the metal bridge, Jackie's Ship Store. My move-in research revealed Jackie Price was the sister of the marina manager, Lester Price.

We'd just made it to the access gate when a slamming door stopped my progress with the key card. "What in blazes are you doing here, you greasy oil slick?"

I'd been called many names in my thirty years, but this was new. "I beg your pardon?"

Lester's burly frame, covered in bib overalls and a dirty T-shirt, barreled toward us. At my question, he stopped and made a surly face before he recognized I was a paying member of the marina. He removed his Houston Texans hat, displacing a mix of black and gray hair that connected to a dirty white beard. "Apologies miss. That scumbag you're with isn't welcome here. That's who I was talking to."

I cast a sideways glance at Jonathan, who sported a satisfied grin. "I'm Ms. Sabatini's guest, so I'll thank you to crawl back in your cave and return to your self-serving ways. If you cared half as much for this lake and marina as you did lining your pockets, maybe more residents would put their boats here rather than a competing marina."

Lester's round, full face flushed an angry red. "I'm going to kill you for being such a pain in my butt!"

Stepping between the two testosterone-fueled men, I smiled and made sure my voice was even and calm in an effort to diffuse the situation. "Surely this can wait until my sunset boat ride is complete. The way the vibrant sun sinks below the surface and, for such a short time, bathes the water in a palette of color just can't be missed." I put my hand on Lester's bicep and the tension ebbed a bit from his body. "I'm certain this score can be settled in another hour or so, right?"

Lester's sigh conveyed resignation and frustration at the same time. "Of course, ma'am. Enjoy your ride. Though, with him, I don't see how that can happen." His gaze narrowed as his lips compressed from the light smile he'd given me to a thin line when he focused on Jonathan. "I'll be waiting for you."

With that unpleasantness behind us, we made our way to the very last dock, the one closest to where the boats left the marina and readied my small speed boat for departure. I didn't say anything until we'd left the no-wake zone. The moment we crossed that buoy, I pushed the throttle forward and we headed into the center of the twenty-thousand-acre lake. I chanced another look at Jonathan to see if he was upset from his encounter with Lester. His head was lifted high, welcoming the wind, and the gleam of his teeth in the light told me he loved being out on the open water as much as I did. He'd left Lester and his threat far behind.

I slowed the boat, and we watched the sun sink below the surface. There was something magical about the way the oranges, purples, and reds melted into the water, creating breathtaking views in the sky and lake.

"It's something, isn't it?" Jonathan's deep voice finally broke our silence.

"Nothing quite like it, especially from this vantage point."

He nodded. "Would you mind dropping me off at home by way of the water? I don't want to give Lester the satisfaction of trying to kill me tonight." He turned toward me and grinned, "Though I'm pretty sure I could outrun his fat—"

"As if he was serious," I laughed. "He's not going to kill you. This is a quiet, peaceful community. There should be no reason for anyone to kill anybody."

"Oh, I've given plenty of people plenty of reasons. Besides you and Kelsey, the only other person here who wouldn't love to see me dead is Ted Birmingham."

"I've heard that name. Isn't he one of the members of the HOA board?" I knew, but I figured the less knowledge he thought I possessed, the more information he'd supply.

Jonathan pointed in the direction he wanted me to go, so I obliged by turning the wheel to head toward a small outcropping near the end of the peninsula that made up the town and community of Wilson. Once satisfied I was going to take him home without forcing him to run through the marina gauntlet, he sat in the seat next to my captain's chair, leaned his head back and slowly exhaled. "My mission since arriving six months ago is to point out to all of these pretentious pansies that their little slice of heaven isn't nearly as angelic as they'd like to think."

"And Lester?"

"Cuts corners that involve the safety of his boaters. I'm pretty sure he's up to some other shady stuff too, but I don't have the proof yet."

I wasn't sure what his endgame was, but proof was always a good thing to have. Though, I'd learned, not always necessary. A confession of wrongdoings was better than proof any day.

Jonathan stood as we neared the area he'd directed me to. "Right there. Just pull alongside the dock, and I'll tie you off."

Usually, I was better able to keep my thoughts to myself, but tonight had taken a lot of interesting turns. "You live in an RV park?" Truthfully, I was embarrassed by the incredulity in my voice.

He chuckled as he stepped out of the boat and offered his hand. Such a gentleman for someone whose main purpose in life was revenge. He gestured to the rows of homes that could pick up and move in thirty minutes or less. "They're all nice and no one pretends to be something they aren't. I like living here because I'm not subject to the rules that govern the homeowners of Wilson."

Recognition dawned. There was, for some unknown reason, a part of the peninsula that the original occupants had decided not to incorporate into the town of Wilson. Because they were unofficial, they weren't subject to the deed restrictions and homeowner association (HOA) rules the rest of the community was. I'd tried to discover why in my research, but I had been unable to learn anything more.

The fact Jonathan chose this area to live in, however, made perfect sense.

"Hey, handsome," a gravelly voice called out from an approaching woman.

Whatever her age, the decades appeared to have been hard on her, though I could see echoes of a beautiful woman remained. Her thin frame was top heavy and her bleached blonde hair sported a ponytail on each side, which seemed incongruent for her age. The ensemble was completed with leather pants and a leopard print halter top. Her cat eyes narrowed as Jonathan slipped his arm around my waist and pulled me closer.

The last thing I wanted was to be any point in a lover's triangle, especially when I was certain this woman would grind me into the ground with her thigh-high boots rather than share anything, or anyone, with me.

"Hey, EZ," Jonathan replied as he leaned in like he was going to kiss me. Once he was close to my cheek, he whispered. "I never forget a face and while you were in disguise during your time in North Dakota, I remember you. How much are you willing to pay for me to keep your secret?" After he asked his question, he moved to kiss me.

I now understood a little better his earlier comment about liking to mess with everyone. While Jonathan's question shook me, I would figure out how to deal with it later. The goal now was to escape and have nothing more to do with him. I slammed my heel down on his foot, then pushed hard. "Never in a million years!" My response was both to me paying him blackmail and him kissing me.

The woman he had called EZ stormed forward and pushed me hard before she went to Jonathan's aid. He was now sporting a satisfied smirk, one I'd like to wipe off his face. I righted myself and headed to my boat. "I think we're done here."

He laughed. "Oh, c'mon, I was just having some fun. EZ appreciates fun and games, don't you?"

"EZ?" I asked, my curiosity winning out for just a moment over my desire to leave these two to whatever plans they might have with each other. Besides, knowledge was power, and, without a doubt, I needed some power over Jonathan.

The woman lifted a cigarette to her lips, took a long draw, and then exhaled in my direction. "Estelle Zimmerman, but some folks like to call me EZ."

"Be truthful," Jonathan teased. "That's not the only reason people call you that, now is it?"

"Well, Ms. Zimmerman, I assure you I have no designs on your man. I was simply giving him a ride home. You can be certain I won't be doing that again." I turned to Jonathan, not wanting to further engage him, but to issue at least one warning. "And Jonathan, you try to kiss me again without an invitation and you'll reap all the benefits of my self-defense classes. Understood?"

He nodded and laughed as he took EZ's hand and started to walk away. He looked over his shoulder. "Don't forget what we talked about, Ms. Sabatini. Thanks for the fun and enlightening evening."

Having had enough *fun* for one night, I decided to take advantage of the dock at the back of my property rather than see Lester again at the marina. Darkness was starting to descend on the lake, but I could still make out some hard-core kayakers taking advantage of what was left of the day. I should have skipped this whole evening and taken my kayak out for a nice sunset paddle.

But eventually, Jonathan would have seen me and

issued his blackmail ultimatum. I'd never been one to run from a bully, and I wasn't going to start now. All that was needed was a good game plan.

Tomorrow promised to be full of potential and excitement. I would use my creative energy to make my store a success and find a way to effectively deal with the Jonathan problem before it got out of hand.

Chapter Two

A normal morning for me consisted of a walk on one of four routes I'd plotted to give me quick access to areas ideal for hiding. One could never be too careful. Familiarizing yourself with your surroundings and knowing all points of exit was key to never getting caught. On the mornings I didn't walk, I took my kayak out onto Lake Amore and watched as the sun made its ascent into the sky and brightened the day.

Instead of either of those activities, I skipped my morning routine altogether, too excited for the opening of my shop. I unlocked the door and smiled proudly at the sign above it: Tesoro, which is Italian for treasure. All around me were carefully chosen Murano and Venetian glass pieces from my father's home country of Italy. It was love at first sight for my parents. She was a nurse, fresh out of college and working for Doctors Without Borders, and my father's family believed in using their wealth to help those less fortunate. This led him to meet the love of his life while delivering supplies to the refugee camp where my mother was working.

My smile continued as I checked each vase, chandelier,

glass, goblet, and item of jewelry to make sure it was positioned just right. I'd painstakingly positioned each beam of light around the shop to ensure each piece sparkled. Three hours later, my smile had faded. Not one person had visited. Not even those who might be curious about a new place to spend their discretionary income. My confidence was shaken. Every venture I'd taken before had been successful. Of course, I'd never pursued an interest on my own behalf. No, it had always been for someone else. Maybe that was what I was destined to do for the rest of my life.

I was about to close for lunch when the bell on the door rang. I hurried to the front. The woman exuded wealth and power. Her attire, black slacks, a red silk blouse, and a black-and-white checked silk scarf, covered her perfect frame. I had no doubt each piece of jewelry and clothing she wore came from only the finest designers and, most likely, had been tailored to fit her perfectly. I didn't know her name but recognized her from the table of people Jonathan and I had taunted last night. "Good afternoon and welcome to Tesoro. I'm the owner, Sadie Sabatini."

"I know who you are." She cut off my attempt at pleasantries. Though only an inch or so taller than me, she'd mastered the art of looking down at those around her.

One more attempt at niceties before my inner witch was set free to circle her head on a flying broom. "Well, Ms. Whoever You Are, as this is our grand opening, I'm offering a ten percent discount to all customers. Anything special you're interested in?"

She closed the distance between us until only a foot or so of space remained. Definitely too close for my comfort. "I am Mrs. Emma Jane Birmingham. My only interest is to warn you I intend to have this space sooner rather than later, so you best not get too comfortable. It was supposed to be mine in the first place. You may think that stunt you pulled last night won you an award, but I know your type. And, if you know what's best, you'll stay away from Jonathan Kirkpatrick as well."

"Or?" I leaned in a little and pulled myself to my full height. If she thought her designer clothes or warnings would scare me off, she would soon learn differently.

To her credit, she didn't flinch or back down. This was obviously a woman who issued commands and expected them to be followed. She also had the resources, I was certain, to make good on any threats issued. She painted a fake smile on her face and glanced at her perfectly mani-cured nails. "Or nothing. Have a nice day, Ms. Sabatini." She turned on her heel and left.

While her comments rattled me, they didn't scare me. Bullies typically were insecure and overcompensating for something missing in their lives—usually love. I needed to find what Emma Jane was missing and try to provide that to her. We'd be besties, then. I laughed out loud. Okay, prob-ably not, but it was worth a try. I truly didn't want to make enemies when I'd just left the last bunch behind.

No longer hungry, I decided to go into my office and do a Google search on Emma Jane Birmingham to see what I might learn. I'd barely powered up the laptop when the bell on the door rang again. I hurried to the front.

Kelsey stepped in.

"Hi! As my first official customer, I'm giving you ten percent off anything in the store."

When I only received a small upturn of the corners of her mouth, I decided to try again. "Okay, you win, fifteen."

This earned me a sad smile. "I wish I was here for shop-ping and chit chat, but I wanted to give you a heads-up."

"About?"

"They found Jonathan's body floating near the entrance to the Wilson Marina."

"What?! You can't be serious?"

"I'm afraid I am. It's so sad. I know he wasn't popular but, in time, people would've come around. I have to believe that."

I appreciated her faith in humans, however, I'd witnessed incredible stubbornness from people many times. "Do they suspect foul play?"

"I haven't heard. Given the circumstances, I'm certain they'll investigate."

Her statement brought into focus why she'd made a visit to share this information. "And you suspect their investigation might lead them to my front door to ask questions."

She nodded. "You two garnered a lot of attention when you left the club last night. Lester also confirms you were at the marina together, and a resident of the RV park says you two had a physical altercation." Her hands went to her round hips and she laughed. "You managed to upset both ends of the social class scale last night. That's a gift."

The stories that news and gossip spread like wildfire in small towns were not exaggerated. Not wanting to play my hand either way, I simply nodded. "I suppose."

Kelsey moved to stand in front of me. Her green gaze stared into my brown eyes for several moments. "I don't believe for one second you were involved. You had no reason to." Then, she faltered a bit. "Right?"

I'd upset countless people over the years, not all of whom I recalled. I still didn't remember Jonathan, but it was obvious he remembered me. He had mentioned North Dakota, so there had to be a connection to the people my team and I had run a con on to get back land and money that rightfully belonged to our client. Justice was blind. I was not.

And the police wouldn't be, either. If Jonathan had told EZ about his blackmail, it was possible she had already told the police. If not, there was no guarantee she wouldn't share in the future. Small towns were quick to judge, especially the new kids on the block. Without a doubt, I was the one they'd judge first. Smiling, I put my hand on Kelsey's arm to convey sincerity. "You're one hundred percent correct. I had nothing to do with any of this. Our so-called altercation was me pushing him away when he tried to kiss me. If I killed every man who tried that without permission, there'd be a lot of sailors who never made it back from shore leave."

She exhaled slowly, relief evident on her face. She nodded. "I knew I was right about you. I'm a good judge of character."

Her marriage to Pete suggested otherwise. Because she'd been so kind to me, I wouldn't disagree and keep her husband on the to-be-determined list. Realizing my time could be limited, I needed to know if she had any more information to share. "Do you have more details I should know before the police arrive?"

She sucked in her bottom lip as her expression became one of deep concentration. After a minute or so, she released it. "I don't know much, and I'm not sure how helpful it will be, but here goes. The game warden retrieved the body after a fisherman called it in. You know they like to fish on the break wall that protects the marina. Even I like to go there from time to time..."

"Kelsey, please. Time is essential."

"Yes, yes. My apologies. The body was delivered to Crockett County Hospital, though I'm not sure why since he had to be dead by the time the fisherman called it in. At any rate, the game warden handed it off to the Wilson police to handle the investigation. I'm sorry, that's all I know right now."

A chuckle escaped despite the circumstances. "Not bad for a few hours' work."

"I'm a well-connected spoke in the gossip wheel." She shrugged. "Is there anything I can do to help you?"

I grabbed my purse, since I'd been about to head to lunch anyway, and ushered her to the door. "You've been very helpful and kind already. I truly appreciate it and consider you my first real friend since moving here. Thank you. I'm going to go home and wait for the police."

The shop was only about seven minutes away from my home on Lake Estates Drive. This stretch of road ran along the endpoint of the peninsula and offered the best lakefront property. I'd splurged a bit, but I'd been moving around my entire adult life, so I decided wherever I called home needed to fit me perfectly. My father, an investment broker/wizard for Berkshire Hathaway, had helped me invest my money wisely. Since this was technically the start of my retirement from my former life, I'd cashed some of those in. The rest of the money...well, some things one just didn't tell her father.

A squad car was sitting at the curb beside my driveway when I arrived home. I pushed the button to open the garage and pulled in. No reason not to follow my normal routine. It wasn't like I was a murderer or anything. While tending to my details, a young man—maybe mid-twenties— left his car and swaggered up my driveway. He was waiting just outside the open door.

Delaying things would only prolong the inevitable, so I walked up to him and smiled. "Good afternoon, officer."

He lifted his cowboy hat, revealing a mop of brown

hair that must have rebelled against any hair products who tried to tame it. "Afternoon, ma'am. Deputy Jake Matthews."

"I'm Sadie Sabatini, Deputy Matthews, but I'm certain you knew that already."

"Ma'am, I'm going to need you to come to the station. The chief would like a word."

"Why?"

"Ma'am?"

I appreciated law enforcement but had learned over the years their adherence to strict rules and protocols made their jobs so much harder. They couldn't always help those who really needed it because they couldn't step outside the black-and-white lines. That was why I had always operated in the gray. "What would your chief like to speak with me about?"

The swagger he'd shown in his step moved right on up his body and appeared as a smirk. "I'm pretty sure you know that already."

Managing to keep my sigh stifled, I nodded. "Yes, of course. Tell me, am I the first stop since I'm the new kid in town? Have you questioned anyone else? When I left Jonathan, he was very much alive."

His face flushed red, and his lips morphed into a thin line. "Don't make me cuff you."

His response seemed over the top. The temptation to lighten the mood by sharing I might enjoy the cuffs hovered on the tip of my tongue. I decided my words were wasted on him. I'd save it for the chief. "Fine. Let me grab my yogurt and I'll meet you at the station."

"I'll wait here."

I left him standing at the entrance to my garage and went inside to grab my lunch. It wasn't much, but probiotics and protein were all a woman with my metabolism could have for lunch and still turn heads at dinner.

Deputy Matthews put away his phone when I exited the kitchen and stepped outside. "You know the way?"

Nodding, I opened the door to my black truck. Normally, the golf cart would work fine, but sometimes a woman needed something faster, and this could prove to be one of those times. "Wilson isn't that big."

A few minutes later, we pulled into the parking lot of the small station. I'd learned this was an annex of a larger department from the neighboring town of Carson and for Crockett County. The small number of residents in this town didn't justify a chief and a deputy in my opinion, but I'm certain it brought the citizens of Wilson a small measure of comfort knowing they were close by.

Chief Seth Parker stood as we entered the building. He was about six feet tall. His muscled frame filled the small room. His cowboy hat sat on the edge of his pristine desk. Closely cut blond hair led to a chiseled jaw. It was too bad he was in law enforcement, otherwise I'd like to spend time with this cowboy.

"Miss Sabatini, please have a seat." He cast a look at Jake. "I'll take it from here."

"But, sir..."

"That will be all." The chief's deep voice left no room for argument.

Heck I might have been willing to follow his instructions if he weren't about to interrogate me.

Once we were alone, he gestured to the chair opposite his desk. "Please, have a seat."

The best defense was always a good offense, I'd learned. I took a seat and started right away. "Besides the fact I'm the new gal in town, do you have any reason to suspect me in this investigation of yours? And are you even sure it's murder? The man apparently liked Jack Daniels. Maybe he slipped and fell into the water. From what I learned in the short time I knew him, he liked to push people's buttons. And some people are very protective of their buttons."

He leaned back and put his hands behind his head, totally relaxed. "Are you?"

"Am I what?"

"Protective of your buttons?" He smiled, revealing a perfectly straight set of white teeth.

He was a little too perfect for my liking. "Why am I here?"

"You were one of the last people to see him alive. Wouldn't you want to talk to that person?"

I crossed my arms and slipped one leg over the other, utilizing body language to send the message that I was about done with this conversation. That, and I wasn't ready to admit the validity of his point too readily. "Perhaps, but I had no reason to kill him."

He leaned forward, his elbows resting on the spotless surface of his desk. "Maybe you do, maybe you don't. I'll know soon enough. To answer your other question, preliminary evidence from the coroner, which I will not share with you at this time, leads us to believe he was murdered rather than taking a Jack Daniel's-inspired tumble into the water. Besides denying involvement, do you have anything else you'd like to share?"

Since I wasn't being arrested yet, and his cool confidence irritated me on multiple levels, I decided to be less than cooperative at that moment. "No. Nothing comes to mind."

His grin told me he didn't believe me, but since he couldn't arrest me and couldn't compel me to share anything more at the present time, he simply stood. "Then, I thank you for your time. I'll be in touch."

I stood and headed for the door.

Before I could make my exit, he added, "Oh, and Ms. Sabatini?"

With a long sigh, I peered over my shoulder. "Yes?"

"Don't leave town."

Chapter Three

After thirty minutes of pacing my sparsely furnished living and dining room combo, I acknowledged there was no way I could wait there and do nothing. Chaos swirled around in my brain, demanding I do something. First things first, I needed to pay Lester Price a visit. I changed into comfy clothes and shoes and grabbed the key to my boat, which was still parked at the dock behind my house. Since I'd skipped my walk earlier, getting my steps in while returning from the marina would accomplish the goals of getting exercise, eliminating some of that extra energy, and focusing my mind.

The ride over to the marina wasn't long, and another pang of jealousy hit me at the kayakers enjoying the late afternoon sun. I'd just purchased a shiny, new bent-shaft paddle I was anxious to get into the water. Instead of focusing on what I was missing, I took in the stately homes, dense trees, and occasional restaurants making up the shoreline. A few deep breaths in and out calmed my unrest. I'd been in worse situations before and emerged unscathed. Nothing would stop me from figuring out who actually killed Jonathan and proving my innocence, even before I was charged.

Once my boat was secured, I walked along the gangway that separated the north and south sides of the slips. I noted some of the decking was worn and several of the water and electrical outlets were marked as out of order. Though I couldn't tell at this time of day, I'd bet money some of the lights were out, too. Maybe Jonathan's accusation about Lester cutting corners was valid. I knew what my slip cost me each year, and it was the least expensive of all the choices because it was the farthest dock from the marina. The location was perfect for me, and the cost saving was a bonus.

The main gate squeaked as it opened, alerting anyone in the near vicinity of someone exiting. Lester came out of the office. The moment he saw me, his visage turned beet red and the scowl left no doubt I served as a primary source for his anger.

"You!" His chubby finger pointed directly at me as he barreled in my direction. His action was unnecessary as I was the only person around.

The moment he got close enough, I grabbed his finger and twisted, forcing his whole body to bend low to ease the pressure. "Yes, me. Now, are we going to talk like two civilized beings, or do I need to break your finger?"

There was some grumbling and cursing under his breath, and at least one word that rhymed with witch. I smiled and applied the tiniest bit more pressure.

It was all he needed. "Okay, okay! Let's talk."

The finger was released, and he took a moment to nurse the tender digit. "Maybe I should call Deputy Matthews and file assault charges against you."

"You could, but as fast as the rumor mill flies around

here, I wouldn't even make it home before word around town was that you got manhandled by little ol' me. Speaking of the rumor mill, I'm sure you've heard Jonathan is no longer a threat to you. Though, the fact he was found at the entrance to *your* marina might give law enforcement a reason to take a closer look at you."

The death glare he shot my way might have given me pause if I wasn't one hundred percent certain I could outrun him. "But that still doesn't explain why you are angry with me." I pretended to think about it for a moment but had suspected there would be a confrontation when I got here. People were predictable. "Unless you're worried that while Jonathan and I were off on our sunset cruise, he might have shared details about why he thinks you're as crooked as they come."

He leaned against the side of the building and crossed his beefy arms, his fingers safely tucked under sweat-soaked armpits. "He had nothing, so you got nothing. And since neither of you have anything, I had no reason to kill him."

I mimicked his stance on the building opposite him, minus the sweaty body parts. "Makes me wonder why you threatened him in front of a witness, then. I mean, if he had nothing, as you say."

"So, was it a lover's spat? EZ told me he tried to kiss you. Or maybe he had something on you. He liked to blackmail people. Pretty sure that's how he came into his money. How else could he afford to live here?"

Despite his attempt at redirection, his fishing expedition landed him a trophy bass. If Jonathan told EZ and she told Lester, any relief I might have experienced at not having to deal with Jonathan's blackmail diminished with the fact there might be two more people interested in cashing in on this deal.

Jonathan had said he liked to mess with everybody, and I now knew that included blackmail. By its very nature, earning money in that manner was a risky business

"Did he try to blackmail you? Or do you know some people he might have blackmailed?"

Lester's belly jiggled as he laughed. If all the hair on his head was white, after a few hours in a shower, he could pass for Santa with the bowl full of jelly merriment from the Christmas story. "First, I'm not telling you anything. You really should be more careful. I'd say you would ruin your reputation, but you ain't been here long enough to have one."

"Well, I'm certainly not taking reputation advice from you, of all people." The petulant sound of my voice irritated me. Typically, I was better at not letting people get under my skin. This man, however, hit all the notes on my aggravation scale.

He pushed off the wall and took the steps necessary to invade my personal space, again keeping his fingers tucked safely behind him. "You better take this advice. Folks here in Wilson look after our own. Outcasts like you and Jonathan don't belong here. Stop sticking that long nose where it doesn't belong."

That kind of hurt. I'd always thought of my nose as being just right. "I kept your name out of my statement to the police, but if they continue to shine the spotlight on me, I will share with them not only that you threatened Jonathan the night he was murdered, but how he also clued me in to his suspicions about you."

Though I expected another threat, he moved back into his own space and smiled, but not in a warm or affectionate way. "Remember my advice."

With his ominous warning, he turned and headed back

into the office. I took advantage of the opportunity to make my exit. The urge to jog or run shouted from the front part of my brain, but the pact I'd made with myself when I was a teenager loomed larger than the booming fear manifesting itself. I'd promised myself never to run, not even if someone was chasing me.

Instead, I held my head high and walked with purpose through the parking lot until I reached Marina Drive. I turned left and followed it all the way until it ran into Main Street. A mile later, I was home and grabbed a glass of wine to aid in my strategy session to figure out my next move.

Sadly, it had only taken a half glass for me to know I had to bring at least one con out of retirement. The Blog Without Borders Con, named in honor of my mother's first job at Doctors Without Borders, would involve me playing the part of an investigative blogger who would question the game warden responsible for the retrieval of Jonathan's body to see if I could learn any more details.

It was at times like this that I wished my team was still together. For this job, I was especially missing my IT whiz kid. She always handled the backstory details and made sure our cover story would hold up under at least moderate scrutiny. The others wouldn't have been needed for this basic con, but I still missed their friendship and advice.

We'd agreed to go our separate ways and not contact each other for at least a year to be safe. The last job we'd pulled together in North Dakota had brought a lot of heat. Our client was vindicated, and the score settled. In the end, that was all that mattered, right?

An hour and multiple watches of two YouTube videos later, I'd created the semblance of a blog journal that covered the basics. It wasn't fancy, but I just needed something there in case they checked out my story. I went to my hidden safe and retrieved a business card for the persona I'd used for the blog. I might have left the "life," but I wasn't discarding all the tools of the trade assembled throughout my years of service to the greater good.

The drive to the Crockett County game warden's office took about thirty minutes. I had no idea what hours this branch of law enforcement worked. An online search would answer my question, but the need to be active and do *something* felt critical at this moment. Driving helped focus my thoughts. Getting the answers in person rather than over the phone allowed me to see the body language and read the face of the person giving me the information. Sometimes, what someone did rather than what they said told the story even better.

I pulled into a complex with three buildings, one in the middle and two on each side. The courtyard in the middle provided a nice colorful contrast to the whitewashed brick of the buildings. The informational sign showed the county jail to be on the right, local government offices in the middle, and the US Fish and Wildlife Service on the left. I backed into a spot closest to the door of the building on the left, grabbed my purse, took a deep breath to get into character, and then headed inside.

The interior of the building offered no surprises and looked exactly as one would expect. Utilitarian walls and offices decorated with pictures of local flora, fauna, lakes, and indigenous animals. Along the main wall of the entryway hung eight-by-ten glossy portraits of those who were serving. One picture in particular drew my attention. Jeremy Raber. The picture captured him standing alongside his boat, smartly dressed in his uniform and wearing a proud smile. It was easy to see he loved his job. For some reason, the smile on his tanned face helped settle my nerves a little more. The sunglasses he wore prevented me from seeing his eyes. How disappointing.

"Can I help you, ma'am?" A warm voice with just a hint of silk brought me out of my study.

I turned and found myself face to face with none other than Game Warden Jeremy Raber. His eyes did not disappoint. Hazel with gold flecks and crinkled with merriment. The in-person version was even better than the photograph.

I couldn't help myself. "Just admiring the view, sir," I flirted.

His laugh, accompanied by a blush and subsequent rubbing of his hand through his short hair, spread warmth through my entire body. I ignored any warning bells my internal alarm system blared in the background of my mind.

"I highly doubt you came here to look at my picture, but thank you for the compliment."

I nodded and, out of habit, flashed my card quickly in front of him. "Sadie Jenkins, reporter for *Motive and Mystery Investigative Blog*. I was hoping to speak to the game warden who retrieved Jonathan Kirkpatrick from Lake Amore this morning."

The smile faded, and I stifled my disappointment. It was for the best, though. Emotions and work didn't combine. Not safely, anyway. Wanting to put the smile back on his face, I added, "I know reporters aren't popular. I had the opportunity to meet the victim and get to know him a little before his demise. This is my way of trying to find out what happened and make sure he gets justice." I gave myself bonus points for telling the truth. It might not have been the whole truth, but it did fit the *nothing but the truth* part.

Jeremy sighed and gestured down the hallway. "I was the person tasked with retrieving Mr. Kirkpatrick. I'm not sure how helpful I can be, but please come to my office and we'll chat for a few minutes."

His office, neat and orderly, gave me a hint into the man with the kindest eyes and smile I'd ever met. At this self-admission, a battle began to rage inside. Pulling off a successful con, even if it was just to get information, required assessing the mark and identifying weaknesses one could exploit to get what they wanted. Everyone had weaknesses that could typically be tied back to love. The love of money, power, or other people. Ironically, those same items meshed well with the primary motives for murder: robbery, jealousy, and vengeance. I suspected Jeremy's weakness was love of people. He was a civil servant, and those eyes...

Not wanting to think any longer in that direction, I ignored my inner romantic, currently being ruled by hormones, and forged on. "I know they found him near the entrance to the Wilson Marina. Do you know the estimated time of death or where he might have fallen into the water?"

His eyes closed as he exhaled slowly through slightly pursed lips. I tamped down emerging thoughts about his lips and stayed focused on the task at hand.

He opened his eyes. "Only the coroner can determine the time of death. Even in a lake, it would be impossible to determine in what area he would have entered the water."

"Do they suspect foul play?" I knew they did since I was at the top of their suspect list.

"That is for the Wilson Police Department and the coroner to determine. I'm sorry, ma'am."

"Please, call me Sadie." And for some reason, I really wanted to be on a first-name basis with him.

"Sadie" he amended, with just a hint of the smile returning. "I'm happy to reach out to Chief Parker over there to see if he would agree to an interview."

No! I wanted to shut that down quickly, but I also didn't want to tip my hand by reacting too negatively to his offer. "You are so kind. Thank you. I'm familiar with law enforcement there. I don't want you to go to any extra effort because of little ol' me." My subconscious survival skills laced my statement with a hint of a Southern accent. It was a proven fact that the accent added to the endearment. I'd earned enough truth points with this visit alone to reward myself with another glass of wine this evening.

He stood, indicating our time together was coming to an end. I searched frantically for something, anything, to say to prolong my stay.

He walked to the door and opened it. "I'm truly sorry, Sadie, that I don't have more to offer. If you want to leave your card, I'll take it, and if I hear anything about the investigation I can share, I'll be happy to reach out."

That was something, and without a doubt, better than nothing. Against my normal protocols, I handed him my card as I joined him at the door. "You've been very kind. Thank you. I'm also sure you handled your job this morning with the utmost of care." I put my hand on his arm, even though I knew I shouldn't. "I can see it in your eyes, the respect you give to all creatures you come in contact with."

Jeremy offered a bashful smile and dipped his head. "Just doing my job."

And I knew he meant it. As I stepped outside his office, the hormone-driven woman broke free from her prison and took charge. Smiling at him, I might have blushed a little since my face heated up a few degrees. "Look, I know you couldn't be of professional help, but I still want to say thank you. Would you have dinner with me one evening?"

He froze for a moment, and I realized the error of my ways. A classy Southern lady would never have taken the initiative to invite him to dinner. I really was out of practice. Finally, the gold flecks in his eyes lit up and his smile returned. "Let me think about it."

Before I could go all schoolgirl-with-a-crush on him, I added, "My number is on the card. Text me if you'd like to go and we'll coordinate the details."

Jeremy nodded and I made my exit before I could say anything more to embarrass myself. In the truck, I leaned my head back and exhaled slowly. I'd totally lost my touch. During my brief time with Jeremy, I hadn't lied once, and I'd put emotions in front of the job. It probably was a good thing I'd retired, otherwise my team would have fired me. At least the card had the number to one of the burner phones I used for cons rather than my normal cellphone.

Speaking of that phone, I pulled it from my purse. I'd had it on silent mode during my time in the warden's office. There were several missed calls from a Wilson area code number and a voicemail. I pressed the symbol to listen to the message and put the phone on speaker.

"Hi, Sadie, it's Kelsey. I'm sorry to bother you, but I had your number from the card you gave me Wednesday night. Pete and I were having a late lunch at the Lakeside Grill and overheard Deputy Matthews bragging to some buddies about Jonathan's case. He said they were about to wrap it up because they'd heard from some of their contacts, and they now had the one thing they'd been missing against you...motive."

Chapter Four

My alarm on Friday morning brought an end to hours of restless sleep. I truly thought the police would be banging down my door in the middle of the night to make their arrest. No one was more surprised than me that I woke up a free woman in my own bed. Maybe Deputy Matthews was just bragging for the boys. It was also possible they didn't see me as a flight risk and Southern manners dictated they didn't disturb the neighbors with such ugly business after ten in the evening. Or, more likely, Chief Parker was getting all his ducks in a row before making his arrest. Regardless, it meant I had a few more hours to work up alternate theories of the crime to present to the chief. He seemed reasonable, unlike his young protégé, Deputy Matthews.

Because I'd ignored my routine yesterday, I decided it was important to resume some normalcy. I wanted people to see me out and about, not hiding like some criminal. I downed my espresso, dressed in my walking clothes, grabbed some water, and headed out. I decided to take the route that would have me encounter as many locals as possible.

The air wasn't stifling yet as it was late May. I put my earbuds in but didn't turn on any music. It was important to be able to listen without people realizing it. Sometimes, you could pick up important details. I headed down Lake Estates Drive until I hit Main Street. Walking with purpose, I kept my head on a swivel and looked for opportunities to engage with the locals. I might have also hoped to see a deer or two. They were prevalent here as there were plenty of wooded lots for them to hang out in. Another reason Wilson was an easy choice for my new home and new life.

About ten minutes later, my route proved to be a good choice when I heard a golf cart stop parallel to where I was waiting to cross the road.

"Well, hello, neighbor. You must be the new gal in town."

I pretended to hit pause on my phone where my music would have been playing, then turned toward the couple and smiled. They looked older than me, but still not as seasoned as some of the residents in Wilson. Maybe their late fifties? "The one and only."

"I'm Karen Bizzy and this is my husband, Richard."

"Have you lived here a long time?" I gestured to the cul-de-sac off the main road. "Maybe we should move the conversation here, so you won't be in the way of traffic?"

Karen laughed. "No one will mind. They all try to stay on our good side, don't they, honey?"

"Yup."

"That's good to know. I'll be sure to try and do that as well." Though I had no idea why, I figured it was best to play along. My gut told me this couple made everyone else's business their business as well. After all, it was even in their name...kind of.

Time for some ego stroking. "I bet you know everyone."

Her chest puffed a bit as she sat up straighter in her seat. "You could say that."

"Since I'm new in town and trying to get the lay of the land and the good people of Wilson, would you be willing to share some of that valuable knowledge with me?" Good thing I had sugar this morning as I was dishing it out in heaping teaspoons now.

Karen smiled like she'd just ensnared another victim in her circle of influence. "Who do you want to know about?"

"Lester Price."

Her expression deflated and she sighed. "Oh, that big lug." She shrugged. "He stays on the radar of the game warden and the EPA, but they've never found anything to pin on him. I almost feel sorry for him."

Sorry was one thing I didn't feel for Lester. "I've met him a couple of times. Neither encounter was pleasant."

"Oh, he likes to blow and bluster a lot, but his bark is worse than his bite. Isn't it, Richard?"

"Yup."

Richard's ability to communicate everything he needed with one word was both impressive and humorous. Somehow, I managed to not allow the laughter bubbling just below the surface to escape. "Good to know. Well, thank you both for the information. Please stop by my shop, Tesoro, later today. It's the grand opening week and I'm offering a ten percent discount, but for you, I'll do fifteen." Figured I'd sweeten the pot, just in case.

"Well, thank you so much, Sadie. You take care of yourself. Richard and I are here to help you get acclimated. We live just off Shady Lane in the big brick house with the privacy fence."

Since I'd never mentioned my name, it was safe to

assume they already knew me and had formed an opinion. What's fair was fair—I'd done the same to them. I'd learned enough about them to know they would always be a good information source. That alone gave me a good reason to keep on their good side. "Thank you both so much. It was nice meeting you, Karen. And you, too, Richard."

"The pleasure was all ours, wasn't it, Richard?"

"Yup."

I didn't laugh, but I did smile. One could only school her responses for so long. "You as well."

Karen pressed the gas pedal and waved. "Toodles."

I finished my walk without seeing another soul. I thought that was odd for a weekday, but since this was only my third Friday here, I didn't have enough data to establish a normal pattern. I just needed a few more weeks. I tamped down the negative feelings that wanted to jump into my brain, warning me I might not get that time.

This was no time for a pity party about the recent turn of events and trouble I found myself in because of my brief association with Jonathan. Increasing my pace, I finished my walk and arrived home. After a shower and getting ready for work, I grabbed a fresh notebook to write down my thoughts and what I'd learned so far. The process always helped me to keep it straight and see patterns sometimes where others did not.

I opened Tesoro promptly at nine. This little boutique had been a dream of mine for as long as I could remember. The displays housed carefully selected pieces of colored art, jewelry, and table settings made with Murano blown glass selected from an artisan in Venice. I smiled, proud that each piece looked brilliant in the strategically placed lights around the store. There was so much beauty here. Hopefully, people would warm up enough to the new girl in town to take a chance and come visit.

While I was waiting, I took out my notebook and jotted down what I'd learned about people and events from the last twenty-four hours—a necessary step in building a profile on them. When my mind drifted to Game Warden Jeremy Raber, I might have stopped writing and spent a few minutes just picturing him and his smile. Oh, I knew there was no place in my life for a romantic relationship. My previous line of work made it necessary to be able to pick up and move at a moment's notice. While I'd left that kind of work behind, or at least was trying to, it could come back to haunt me at any moment. It would be selfish of me to connect with someone and then leave in the middle of the night to keep them safe. Of the many people and things I'd pretended to be over the years, selfish was never one of them.

The bell on the door rang, dragging me out of my thoughts. A young teen with thick, black hair and a beautiful smile walked in. "Good morning, and welcome to Tesoro."

He walked right up to me and extended his hand. "Morning, ma'am. My name is Emerson Romano. My apologies for not being able to visit you yesterday and officially welcome you to the neighborhood. After finishing up the current school year, I've been helping my aunt in her shop with all the Memorial Day orders."

My hand extended to shake his as my smile widened. Such a southern gentleman with his manners and helping his aunt. "Well hello, Emerson. It sounds like you've been very busy, indeed. I'm glad you were able to find some time to stop by. Would you like to have a look around?"

Emerson nodded, and after glancing over the contents

of the entire shop, walked over to a Murano glass fish sculpture the color of water, both light and dark blue hues. The silver leaf accented the murine details creating a beautiful hand-blown piece.

"Do you like that one?" I was curious as he appeared lost in thought as he studied the fish.

"My mother had one like it. She loved Murano glass."

His use of the past tense did not escape me. "She had a wonderful eye for art, then, as this is one of my favorites as well. Had she traveled to Italy at some point?"

Emerson turned from the sculpture, his dark eyes glistening with unshed tears. "She was born there. My father met her while he was vacationing. Love at first sight, they told me."

"My Papà and Mamma met in a similar way, except they were both working. Also love at first sight. Were you born in Italy?"

He shook his head, clearing away some of the dark clouds over his head. "No, they came to America for their jobs. I was born here."

"Me, too. I'm glad to have found someone in Wilson who will appreciate all things Italian."

"There's not many of us here," he laughed.

"Then, perhaps we can be friends?" The good Lord knew I could use a few, and I would be willing to wager the sculpture that everyone who met Emerson liked him. I decided not to press him any further about his parents. He would tell me when he was ready.

He nodded. "I like the sound of that. I'll introduce you to my Aunt Isabella. She owns Wilson's Flower Shop just two doors down from here."

"I would like that very much. Thank you, Emerson."

"My pleasure, ma'am. If there's anything you need or want to know around here, I'm your guy."

"Is that so? Do you live here or just stay the summers with your aunt?"

The light dimmed in his eyes, and I could have kicked myself. I assumed his mom had died, but that his father was still alive. From the look on his face, that had been a definite miscalculation. "I'm sorry, Emerson. I didn't mean..."

He exhaled slowly. "It's okay. You couldn't have known. My parents died in a boating accident about a year and a half ago. I've lived with my aunt ever since. Even though I'm fourteen, people around here treat me like a community kid. Everyone knows me and helps my aunt since she's by herself. She calls it co-parenting."

I had no idea how old his aunt was, but I couldn't imagine raising a teenager would be an easy task, even one as polite and well-mannered as Emerson appeared to be. Wanting to distract him and put some of the light back in those dark chocolate eyes of his, I decided to enlist his help. "I'm so sorry about your parents. Any time you want to talk about them or hear stories about Italy, let me know. My parents regale me with tales about my father's homeland every visit. In the meantime, might you be willing to help me with something?"

"What do you need? I usually help my aunt in the shop over the summer for at least a few hours a day, but I could help you, too."

I waved my hand around the empty space. "Oh, I think I can handle the throngs of customers."

The one-sided uptick of his mouth transformed into the smallest of smiles. "They'll come around. They're good people. They just need to get to know you. I can help with that."

He was right. I battled with myself about how well I wanted them to get to know me. Not because I was opposed to the idea, but history had taught me a painful lesson. Knowing me could be dangerous for an average run-of-the-mill citizen. "I was hoping you could help me get to know some of them."

His face lit up. "What or who do you need to know?"

I shared with him about meeting Lester and the Bizzys, then handed him a blank notebook out of my bag. "Do you think you could write down what you know in this notebook? It's easier for me to collect and organize my thoughts if they're written down."

"I have a lot of thoughts on Lester that I'll be happy to write down for you. I'll also see what I can learn about the Bizzys."

"Please be careful. I don't want you getting into any trouble on my account."

Emerson laughed and pointed to his dimples. "People love this face. They tell me things. And because of my age, they don't think anything about talking around me. I pay attention."

"Good to know." I smiled. "Thanks for your help, Emerson. Want to meet me here for lunch tomorrow? My treat. I'll make something Italian for you."

"That would be awesome! Thanks, ma'am."

"Sadie," I corrected. If he and I were working together, I didn't need to feel ancient by being called ma'am every time we talked. I knew it was out of respect, but Emerson was shaping up to be my second real friend in Wilson, so we needed to be on a first name basis.

His smile melted my heart. "Thanks, Sadie. See you tomorrow." He cast one last look at the fish and then headed out the door.

After another couple hours of busying myself with making and organizing my notes, I was ready for lunch when the bell jingled again. It was my other friend. "Hey, Kelsey."

"Hi, Sadie. How's business?"

"Same as yesterday, except no visit from the police yet." Might as well make a joke of it until it wasn't anymore. I noticed Kelsey didn't seem as chipper as her normal self. "How are you doing?"

She sighed and plopped down on one of the padded stools next to a display case. "Pete's in a bad mood. Has been since Thursday morning."

"He seemed fine Wednesday night. I don't know him well, but his mood didn't come across as bad."

"Oh, he was plenty happy Wednesday night. Besides happy hour, he went over to the Birminghams that evening for poker night."

"Which Birminghams?" They were a very prominent family and owned several homes here in Wilson. It was important I understood which branch of that family tree we were talking about.

Kelsey huffed. "Emma Jane and Ted, of course. I swear, Pete uses any excuse he can to be near that woman. He also likes to hob knob with her husband and the other powers that be here in Crockett County."

That explained why Kelsey was upset, but not really why Pete would be. "Why is he upset? Did he lose a lot of money on poker night?" I figured I'd steer the conversation away from Emma Jane.

She stood abruptly and began to pace around the store. I prayed she didn't knock over any of the pieces. "He's upset at me. I tend to be very curious."

Translation: nosey. "Go on."

"I was straightening up his office and I saw real estate papers. He was trying to work out a deal for the vacant lot across from us."

So far, this didn't seem worthy of the level of upset she was experiencing. "Did you not want him to buy it?"

"Oh, he's been talking about buying it for weeks now. He told me he was trying to negotiate with the owner but wasn't having much luck. Pete doesn't take no for an answer."

"Who was the owner?"

"He wouldn't tell me, but I saw the papers Wednesday night when I was home alone."

"And?" If Chief Parker thought I was a difficult subject to interrogate, he'd never tried getting an answer out of Kelsey.

She stopped pacing and her gaze pierced the distance between us, telling me more than the two words she uttered. "Jonathan Kirkpatrick."

Chapter Five

Kelsey's revelation certainly added another name to the list of suspects I was compiling. The fact I didn't trust Pete any farther than I could throw him didn't help his case, either. I gestured to the stool she'd been sitting in earlier. "Have a seat and let's talk this through. I'm sure it's just circumstantial."

Her expression conveyed she didn't believe me, but she took the seat anyway. "Tell me what you saw and what happened."

She nodded and exhaled slowly. "As you may or may not know, Jonathan's main residence was in the RV park in the unincorporated part of Wilson."

"I did know that, yes." I didn't understand it, but I knew it.

"What you might not realize is that in order to take advantage of the amenities here in Wilson, you have to be a property owner."

She waited as I processed this. Finally, it came to me. "If Jonathan sold that property to Pete, he would lose his access."

"Yes."

"And given what I've learned about his reason for being here, that access, including voting rights on community matters and board members, would be very important to him."

"Exactly."

"Why would Pete say Jonathan was negotiating with him, then? I can't imagine him giving up the property, no matter the price, given those facts. Unless he owned another lot?" If he didn't, just the little bit I'd already learned about Jonathan told me it would snow in July here before he would sell.

Her shrug told me she wasn't really invested in getting to the bottom of this. "Pete loves negotiating and overcoming objections. He had to think there was a chance or he would've moved on."

"What time did he get home Wednesday night?" This piece of information was more important to me than the rest. Establishing a timeline was critical.

No longer interested in our conversation, Kelsey got up and started looking around at the different sculptures. It only took a moment before the beaded glass bracelets captured her attention. She carefully lifted a gold and aquamarine piece into the area the spotlight covered. Turning it carefully, she appeared absorbed in all the intricate details and craftsmanship. I know I had been, which is why I selected it for the collection. "This is beautiful."

"Thank you. Everything is either Venetian blown glass or Murano glass jewels from my father's home country of Italy." I allowed her a few more moments of studying it before I tried again. "Kelsey?"

"Hmm?"

"The time?"

She looked at her watch and I had to fight back a small twinge of exasperation. "It's almost noon."

"The time Pete got home Wednesday night?"

"Oh, I'm not entirely sure, but it was right around midnight. The poker game started a little after happy hour ended."

I made a mental reminder to add that to my notes. Learning the time of death would be critical to establishing the timeline. Not having a contact at the police department...*or a hacker who could tap into their systems and learn the information*...was a definite drawback to my "turning over a new leaf" life. I'd have to do it the old-fashioned way. Maybe my handsome game warden would have that information if he agreed to have dinner with me. I smiled, thinking of all the ways I might get him to tell me, none of which had anything to do with running a con.

The bell jingled and all my pleasant thoughts were thwarted by the image of Pete coming through the door. His jaw was clenched and the veins in his neck were making an appearance. Though I doubted it, maybe seeing Kelsey surrounded by all this beauty would improve his mood. One could always hope. "Hello, Pete."

His attention shifted from his wife over to me and his frown turned upside down into a forced smile. He walked over to me and took my hand to shake it. I noticed his knuckles appeared as though they'd been through a fight. "Hello, Sadie. How's business?"

I continued to hold his hand, turning it so we could both see the marks. "Pretty standard for the new kid in town." I lifted his hand to display the marks I noticed. "What happened?" Might as well get right to the point.

He pulled away and shrugged. "Working out in the

backyard, wrestling some lawn furniture." He looked at his hand and grinned. "Guess the furniture won."

Even if Kelsey's look hadn't given him away, I would've known he was lying. I'd seen enough fights to know what the injuries looked like afterward. I decided not to comment any further. "Are you here to buy your wife a gift? She's been eyeing that bracelet over there."

His lips pressed together, and he rewarded my question with a frown, but rather than answer me, he walked over to her and slipped his arm around her waist. "You like that one, baby?"

Despite her earlier irritation with him, the way she melted into his embrace made me wonder about their relationship. Maybe he wasn't one hundred percent the jerk I'd originally thought. I wasn't going any lower than ninety percent, though. Maybe he reserved the good ten percent for his wife?

Kelsey nodded and smiled at him. He took the bracelet and handed it to me. "Ring us up."

Jerk or not, he was my first customer and I wasn't going to turn down a sale. Besides, I knew how beautiful the bracelet would look on her wrist, and as the hub in the wheel she mentioned earlier, Kelsey would tell everyone where she got it. Word of mouth advertising from the center of the information (or gossip) hub... it didn't get any better than that. After he paid, I handed him the bracelet. "Why don't you do the honors?"

Pride surged in my heart as I watched him wrap the bracelet around her wrist and connect the clasp. She held it up in the light and her smile made everything I'd been through in the last twenty-four hours or so fade into the background. This...this was my new passion.

Jonathan's face peered at me through the shadows, and I

sighed. This would be my new life if I could survive being the prime suspect in a murder investigation.

A crushing hug brought me from my musings. "Thank you, Sadie." Then, she whispered in my ear, "For everything."

"It's my pleasure. You two have a great day, and tell everyone where you got that bracelet!"

She laughed as they walked, hand in hand, out the door. "Don't worry. I will."

After they left, I went to the back and pulled another piece from the safe, one that would work perfectly in the spot my first sale had just vacated. Once I'd tended to business, I returned to my notebook and put down what I'd learned:

Jonathan owned property in Wilson proper – lot across from Kelsey and Pete.
Pete wanted to buy property. I assume Jonathan toyed with him, but no intention to sell.
Pete was at Ted & Emma Jane Birmingham's playing poker the night Jonathan was murdered.
Allegedly playing poker.
Pete came home around midnight with evidence he'd been in a fight.
Kelsey says Pete doesn't take no for an answer.

Wanting to be thorough, I went ahead and reviewed my other notes:

Jonathan's mother moved from Wilson when she was pregnant with him.
Jonathan made many enemies in the months he'd lived in Wilson.

Enemies included: Lester Price

After a little more thought, I added:

Enemies included: Lester Price, Pete Jensen (?)

Sadly, this was not enough, yet, to create an alternate theory to the crime. It did at least give me another suspect to toss under the proverbial bucking bronco if the police came calling before I could learn more.

A few more residents came in to look around. Though no purchases were made, I could see appreciation for the craftsmanship. That could mean future sales. I handed out my card and wrote a note on each that the ten percent off sale would remain open for those who came in during the grand opening. It warmed my heart that the rumor mill hadn't tainted everyone in the town about me.

The next few hours passed by with me doing various Google searches trying to learn more about incorporated versus unincorporated Wilson and checking local news sites to see if any more information about Jonathan's death had been shared. My search results matched the rest of the day's sales. A big, fat nothing.

Once home, I decided to take advantage of beautiful Lake Amore and the new paddle for my kayak. Sure and steady strokes took me out toward the middle of the lake. As I studied the reflection of trees from the Sam Houston Forest that lined a good portion of the lake's surrounding area, the sun began its journey lower. I couldn't help but feel my soul restored from the beauty of nature. Being around water brought me a calm and sense of inner peace that nothing else had. It also cleared my mind.

The only way to learn more about Jonathan was to go to

the source. Since the source was gone, the next best thing was to understand his life. Where he lived. Who he associated with. A steady sense of purpose served me well as I stroked my way toward the boat dock I'd taken Jonathan that fateful night. The night he'd threatened blackmail. The night he was killed. The night that brightened the unyielding spotlight of attention on me far more than I'd ever wanted.

Maneuvering my way to where I could see the RV park but still a safe distance so as not to appear too nosey, I studied the layout the best I could in the waning light. Three rows of RVs parked with an adequate amount of space in between. A circular gravel drive provided access to each row and easy in-and-out for every person there. It was quiet, clean, and gave off a sense of community as people sat in lawn chairs out in their "yards" and visited with their neighbors while others milled about. Some fire pits were going. It reminded me of camping when I was younger.

The sound of a small engine getting closer tore my focus away from my study. Not that I thought I would recognize anyone, but it was worth a shot. It wasn't unusual to hear an engine. It was a lake, after all. Boats and jet skis were very common and a part of life around here.

The noise got closer and closer. I couldn't help but turn a bit in the water so I could see what was going on. Adrenaline spiked and my heart pounded in my chest as I realized the jet ski was headed directly for me. I grabbed the orange flag that had been in its rightful place on the stern and began to wave it frantically. Boats used it to indicate there were swimmers in the water. As I tended to sometimes sit and watch while I was kayaking, I had it added to mine to indicate my presence and help people avoid me.

This universally accepted signal was obviously not working.

I tossed the flag into the cockpit and began paddling fervently toward the dock. Despite my efforts, the buzz of the engine grew louder and louder until it was all I could hear other than the thundering beating of my heart. The death grip on my paddle added to the numbness spreading throughout my body.

So close...

A few seconds more and I would be near enough to the dock to at least try and get out.

A moment later, time paused as I felt the jet ski turn right behind me, creating a wake that I couldn't accommodate for. My kayak tipped over in the deep water. I sucked in a large amount of air right before I went under. The dark water surrounded me, and I fought the natural urge to panic and thrash around in an effort to right myself.

I forced my brain to slow and encouraged my heart to do the same. My breath continued to hold as instinct and training kicked in. I performed the steps necessary to disengage myself from the kayak. Once free, I broke the surface of the water with a gasp, gulping in precious oxygen. One arm rested on the overturned kayak, holding me afloat in the water. It was going to be a bear getting it flipped back over, emptied out, and then back home again. The fading sound of the jet ski told me my assailant was long gone.

"Here. Grab hold!"

The gravelly voice was easily recognizable, but I was in no position to be choosy. The long pole was connected to a fishing net. On the other end of my rescue pole was none other than Estelle "EZ" Zimmerman. Color me surprised. I took the lifeline she was giving and let her pull me and my kayak the rest of the way to the dock. Once there, I was able to hoist myself up onto the structure. Laying down on my stomach, I grabbed the edge of my kayak and, with considerable effort, got it flipped right side up. My brand new bent-shaft paddle was floating nearby. "Mind if I borrow that?" I asked as I pointed to the fishing net that had aided in my rescue.

EZ handed it to me, and I used it to fish the paddle over close enough to reach it. Once everything was secured, I sat down heavily and looked up at my rescuer. "Thank you."

"You're welcome."

"Any chance you saw who provided my first dunk in the lake?"

She shook her head and pulled out a cigarette, lighting it up. After a couple of draws, she added. "You're attracting enemies faster than mosquitos to fresh blood."

I chuckled at the image that conjured up. "I swear that is the opposite of what I'm trying to do. Apparently, the list is long and unknown to me." Of course, the one enemy I knew I'd made was now dead, so there's that.

EZ finished her cigarette while I caught my breath and tried to think who might try to drown me. She put out the cigarette and walked over to the corner of the dock to put it in a small coffee container that had been repurposed, I'm assuming, for an ashtray. She sat down next to me. "While you catch your breath, let me give you the four-one-one on at least one person on that list."

I had no idea why she was being so nice to me, but I was going to take it. Besides, I really did need to catch my breath before I tried to empty the water from my kayak. "Deal."

"The shop you're in had been earmarked for a special pet project by none other than Emma Jane Birmingham."

"Her, I've met. I was under no illusion she liked me, but I didn't realize she considered me an enemy."

EZ's laugh turned into a full-blown smoker's cough. Once she finished and caught her breath, she resumed the storytelling. "Emma Jane is not a fan of anyone who stands in the way of what she wants or what she'd like to do. She'd whipped the ladies' association into a frenzy about what they could do with the space, but then she dropped the ball when she didn't complete the necessary paperwork in time to do the deal."

Recognition dawned. "Then, I made an offer and closed the deal in record time." I was the kind of person who, once I knew what I wanted, went for it. Wholly and completely. It was both a blessing and a curse at times.

EZ nodded and pulled out another cigarette. "It was an embarrassment to her, both personally and socially."

A sigh escaped me. "So, now I'm public enemy number one as far as she's concerned."

Another nod confirmed my statement. Since she was being so forthcoming, I figured I'd ask the next question on the tip of my tongue. "And is she having her flock of seagulls boycotting my shop as a result?"

"She would never be so obvious. But her...what is it you called them, flock of seagulls? They know enough about survival in that circle to not even darken the doorstep of your shop much less buy something." Her statement was followed by that deep, gravelly chuckle I'd come to associate with her.

"Well, I promise you I'll never be a part of that flock, but I'm hopeful I can win a few of them over in time. Or, if not them, maybe those who just hang out with the other birds on the wire." My analogy was thin, but hey, I'd had my life threatened a short time ago.

"Do you think Emma Jane was behind what happened

here tonight?" I watched her face carefully as I waited for an answer.

A long stream of smoke escaped her lips as she exhaled. "Not really her style, but I've learned people are capable of just about anything."

There was a question burning in my brain that I had to ask, though it might destroy the thin web of truce EZ and I had just formed. "How do you know so much about the elite crowd? No offense, but you don't strike me as a martini at happy hour kind of gal."

Her sharp gaze cut through my words, which made me instantly regret them. Damn that endless curiosity of mine. A moment later, her features softened, but the hard look in her eyes remained. "Where I work, the elite show up and pretend to be someone else for a while. Once they relax, it loosens their lips, and they talk. They typically don't think of people like me as smart enough to understand what they're saying, if they even think we're listening."

"Where do you work?"

EZ stood and deposited another finished cigarette in the coffee can. "Let me help you get the water out of your kayak so you can go home."

Since I wasn't going to turn down her help, I let her non-answer about work slide. "Thank you."

A few minutes later, we'd managed to get the kayak emptied out and put me back in it. I met her gaze and offered gratitude again. "Seriously, thank you for your help tonight."

She shrugged. "Us folks here," she gestured to the RV park, "believe in helping out our fellow man or woman as the case may be."

I nodded in acknowledgement, saddened that not everyone felt the same way. "Can I ask you one more question as long as it doesn't pertain to how you earn your living?"

Her slight smile and nod gave me courage to ask the other burning question in my mind. "Why didn't you tell the police the whole truth about the altercation between Jonathan and me the night he died? Most importantly, that it was a misunderstanding and that he was very much alive when I left."

EZ backed away from the edge of the dock where she'd been standing and retrieved another cigarette. "Because, if they had, they would have known I was not just watching from a distance. They would have realized I was the last person to see him alive."

Chapter Six

EZ's confession gave me much more to think about. I thanked her again for the help and paddled my way home. I did it quickly as the sun had managed to set while I was fending off the jet ski attack and learning more about my neighbors. My pasta dinner had been waiting patiently for me to heat and eat it, which I did. I'd burned a lot of calories over the past hour or so. This meal had been earned.

After dinner and a shower, I couldn't get EZ's words out of my head. I grabbed my notebook and added what I'd learned.

Emma Jane Birmingham – influential in society, especially ladies' association
Emma Jane blames me for her pet project not taking off.
Was EZ really the last person to see Jonathan alive?
Pete has a thing for Emma Jane.

The last one was my own observation. I believed he loved Kelsey, but being around Emma Jane obviously made him feel important. I had no idea how any of that, except my original thoughts about Pete not being able to buy the lot from Jonathan, had anything to do with the murder. Sometimes, things could be connected in ways we couldn't initially see, so it was best to take note.

Which led me back to EZ. She was somehow tuned in to the elite in our area, and I wanted to know how. A quick check of the clock revealed it was nine. I had no idea what time EZ went to work, but I wanted to at least try to see if I could follow her and learn more. I dressed all in black. Though I had no idea where the evening would take me, I knew black was the best color to blend into the night. Besides, it also made a girl look thinner. I never minded that.

Before I could head out, my phone rang with an incoming video call. My parents. Not wanting to miss my opportunity with EZ, but also knowing not taking a call from them would set them both worrying, I swiped up to answer. "Ciao, Mamma and Papà."

"Ciao, Sadie. How's the new business?" With my father's background in business and finance, he'd offered to invest in my newest venture. I'd gracefully turned him down, but he was still keen to see if I was successful or not.

"Slow, but sure. Had my first sale today. You know how it is when you're in a new market." Figured that was easier than trying to explain moving into Small Town USA where no one knew you and it took time to earn their trust.

"That's why you should have opened your shop in Houston."

"Enough, Stefano. Leave her be. She has always been successful in all her endeavors. This will be no different."

"Thank you, Mamma. How are things at the VA center?" My mother had used her nursing degree to help the underserved the moment she got it, from her first gig with Doctors Without Borders to now working at the VA clinic in Omaha where the rest of my family lived.

"Doing what we can each day to try and make a difference. You know how it is."

I did. That's what I'd spent my entire life doing, just in a different way than she had. "You do good work."

She beamed at my praise. I couldn't help but notice my father's adoring expression and the love so clearly displayed in his gaze when he looked at my mother. That was the kind of love I wanted some day—once my new life was established and I could be confident my past was far behind me and would cause no danger to my present. Despite the reasons for doing what I did had always been honorable and helped the people who needed it most, those who were caught in their web of lies and deceit did not look so kindly on my efforts.

My mother nodded at my comment, but then her gaze narrowed as she looked directly at me. "So, tell me, Sadie. You just turned thirty. When are you going to settle down and give me grandchildren?"

"Who's being a pest now, Delaney? Leave her be. She'll settle when she's found someone as wonderful as her father. Then, they will make beautiful babies for us."

These two. I chuckled. "Both of you need to stop worrying about me. We'll have a call this weekend and I'll tell you all about my business plan, Papá. And Mamma, I will tell you all about a handsome game warden I met. Agreed?"

Their matching grins warmed my heart. "Agreed."

Before I let them go, I needed one thing. "Papá, can I ask a favor?"

"Anything, bella."

"I met a man a couple days ago who recently came into

a lot of money. I'm curious how. His name was...*is* Jonathan Kirkpatrick. I think he might be from the North Dakota area, or at least have connections there. Can you see what you can find out?" My father worked as an investment banker at Berkshire Hathaway. He'd been in international business and had connections all over the world. If anyone could find this information out in a legitimate way for me, it was my father.

His look was laser focused as though he were trying to see into my soul and determine the true reason I'd asked. I'm sure he suspected there was more to my request. But fathers had a tough time denying their daughters anything. Mine was no different. "Yes, for you, my beautiful girl, I will see what I can find out."

"Thank you. Ti amo."

"Ti amo."

The call ended with me only feeling slightly guilty for using my father and delaying giving my mother a grandchild. It wasn't like I was the only child they had. Hopefully, they were giving my sister equal grief.

I hurried to my vehicle, a black Ford F150. Hey, when in Texas...

I had no idea what time EZ had to report for work, but it wasn't like I had anything else to do tonight. And my time was limited. The police could show up to arrest me at any moment. It still bugged me they hadn't. What could they be waiting for?

I parked in a cul-de-sac that would give me a view of the RV park. Thankfully, it was well lit so I could make out the drivers entering and exiting. Not much traffic on the side street. Peaceful even. I only had to wait about thirty minutes to see EZ's recognizable pigtails behind the wheel of a Toyota 4Runner. I waited until she turned onto the feeder street leading her to the one road that went in and out of Wilson. Being on a peninsula had its advantages. Only one way in and one way out. Of course, that was also a disadvantage if you needed multiple exit strategies. Hence my boat at the marina. While it would be more convenient to keep it at the dock at my house, the marina offered an unexpected way for me to escape to another area of the lake if I ever needed it. I hated to have to live that way, but it had been all I'd known for years now. I'd learned the hard way that multiple exit strategies were necessary.

Because of the lateness of the hour and my tinted windows, I wasn't too worried EZ would realize I was following her. I maintained a reasonable distance behind her and followed the speed limit. Once out of the peninsula, the road opened to four lanes, but we both maintained our speed and distance. I knew why I didn't want a run-in with the cops, but I wasn't sure about EZ. Maybe she was just a law-abiding citizen?

After five miles, we reached the highway. We turned right and continued another ten miles. Once outside of town, business was sparse with plenty of the wide open spaces The Chicks sang about in between. Finally, a building with a flashing neon sign advertising "The Foxy Lady" came into view. EZ turned into the parking lot. I slowed to give her time to show me where she was headed. Maybe she'd missed her turn? Maybe she was pulling over for a cigarette?

She drove around to the back of the building, so I had the opportunity to pull into the parking lot as well. I waited for as long as I could stand, which wasn't long, then made my way around to the back. Parking as far away from the doors as possible to not draw attention to myself, I watched as more vehicles arrived. Based on how they were dressed and the type of establishment that one would guess The Foxy Lady to be, I determined there was one door for employees and another for guests. There was also a door at the front of the building so I couldn't be sure of my conclusion.

A knock on my left startled me. Having no way to delay the inevitable, I rolled down the window. "Yes?"

"Ma'am, can I help you?"

"Uh, no, I don't think so." Because I hadn't known where EZ worked, and I'd been distracted since our arrival, I hadn't come up with a plausible cover story. Besides, who knew there was security *outside* an adult dance venue? That sounded nicer to say than strip club or another crude descriptor.

His gaze swept over what he could see of my body in the beam of his flashlight and the illumination provided by the parking lot. His smile softened. "Look, if you're trying to find work, you should go to Houston. The clientele here prefers our old timers and fan favorites. You'd make a lot more money in the city."

Part of me wanted to kiss him for implying I was too young to work here. At thirty, I wouldn't think of myself as too young for many activities, especially when it came to this profession. As I thought about it, though, EZ had taken good care of her body. She was strong, thin, and had curves in all the right places. She must be a legend around here.

Realizing he was waiting for me to respond, I donned my best irritated Southern lady face (whatever that locked like) and answered, "Well, I thank you, sir, for the compliment. However, I followed my husband here to learn if he was lying to me about picking up another shift so we could go on that cruise we've been talking about."

The guard offered a sympathetic smile. "Sorry, ma'am.

No married men work security here, so he must be a client. If he pulled around here, then I'm sorry to inform you that he's a VIP, which means he spends a good deal of time and money here."

My huff of disgust was sincere at all the lying men who were probably in there right now. "Well, that explains why we haven't been able to afford that cruise." I batted my eyelids for good measure. "Thank you for the information and your time. I'm sorry to have kept you from your rounds."

"No problem, ma'am. I'm sorry to deliver the bad news."

"It's alright." I winked. "I have a prenup."

He laughed and backed away from the truck to allow my escape. Waving as I rolled up the window, I headed back to Wilson. I now understood why EZ hadn't wanted to share with me where she worked. It also explained how she had an "in" with the elite. It was reasonable to assume some of those elite escaped the monotony of their everyday lives for some fantasy. EZ had mentioned that they had loose lips and shared information. Of course, she'd followed that statement with the all-too-sad understanding this was because they didn't think someone of her standing would be smart enough or even care enough to listen or comprehend. They'd obviously underestimated EZ. I would not make that mistake. She'd seemed close with Jonathan, but she was also the last person—that I knew of, anyway—to see him alive. That had to mean something. Either she killed him or...she wasn't the last person he met on that fateful night.

Chapter Seven

The next morning came as a bit of a surprise. I was still a free woman who'd been allowed to complete her morning routine without interruption. I opened Tesoro promptly at nine and checked every piece to ensure it was displayed perfectly. Before I could make my espresso and find a way to kill time until lunch, my burner phone dinged with an incoming text. My pulse jumped to attention. I only used that phone number when I ran cons. Until the other day, I hadn't done that in the year since I'd left that life behind.

A few deep breaths later, I pulled the phone from the hidden compartment in my purse and looked at the display. *Hi, you still want to have dinner? Jeremy.*

My handsome game warden with the eyes that made me forget all the rules of running a con. I most definitely shouldn't have dinner with him, but oh, how I wanted to. After a few calming deep breaths, I replied. *Of course. Tonight at 7? You choose the place.*

Francesca's on 242.

The man picked Italian cuisine. He might be my soulmate. *I'll be there.*

I returned the phone for safekeeping; grateful I'd not taken the time to return it to the safe after the con. It must be my mother willing the universe to find me a husband and give her that coveted first grandchild. Or, more likely, the universe taunting me with a life that couldn't be mine...at least not for a long time. By then, I'd probably be too old for children.

Sipping my espresso gave me something to do as my mind played over the million scenarios that might occur when I saw Jeremy tonight. They ranged from pure delight to utter destruction and everything in between. Hey, an active imagination was not something I was lacking in. Thankfully, around ten o'clock, a couple of ladies walked in. Then, a couple more. It was the equivalent of a mad rush compared to the number of patrons I'd had thus far. "Welcome, ladies. I'm Sadie Sabatini, purveyor of this fine store. All the items here are authentic designs composed of Murano or Venetian glass from Italy." I moved to the first display case. "Here, we have vases and glassware." I picked up a beautiful piece that had dark blue and gray color etched into the glass in a design that reminded me of seaweed floating free in the ocean. "This set of traditional Venetian glasses would make a great addition to your home and no doubt be a conversation piece at your next party."

They looked interested, so I continued the tour, highlighting my favorites in each display case. After a few minutes, I left them to shop and went back to my stool behind the counter. A small sigh escaped as a wave of disappointment crested over me. Their covert glances and hushed conversations appeared to center more around me than on the works of art they were surrounded by.

Deciding determination rather than disappointment

suited me, I plastered a smile on my face and marched into the den of wolves. I suspected, though, Emma Jane had sent them here to do some reconnaissance, which made them more sheep than wolves. My original assessment of seagulls had been misguided, for sure. However, at the end of the day, they were women just trying to fit in. I could work with that.

I walked up to the one I suspected was the leader of the sheep and extended my hand. Her long, blonde hair flowed easily past her shoulders. She was around my height, maybe an inch taller, with a medium build. She carried herself with her head held high, chin slightly lifted with an upright posture that would make you believe she had a steel rod for a spine, but her eyes gave her away. They were a soft blue, which hinted at a vulnerability and tenderness that led me to believe under the tough exterior was a woman who cared about others. Of course, that conclusion made me wonder why she was part of Emma Jane's crew. "Thank you for coming in today, Ms...?"

She took my hand and returned the greeting. "McDowell. Denise McDowell."

"Ms. McDowell, nice to meet you. Any particular piece calling for your attention?" I watched her and the other minions closely as I waited to see how she would respond.

She pointed to the stemware section. "That black goblet with the golden stem is quite remarkable."

"Indeed, it is. You have a very good eye."

Her chin lifted even more as she made an effort to look down on me with a disapproving stare. "Rather pricey, though, don't you think?"

I pretended to give her assessment some consideration before I responded. "Manipulating the glass into the proper shape and strength requires talent and years of training. Additionally, the gold is solid and pure, not plated. As such, at three hundred dollars, it's quite a steal. However, I'm willing to make you a deal."

"I'm listening."

My heart fluttered as I could see she really was. She might have come here on an alternate mission, but beauty is beauty and she recognized it. "For every name and possible motive you or your friends can provide me with of people who might have had a beef with Jonathan Kirkpatrick, I'll give you another five percent off the cost."

This had them murmuring and moving to talk amongst themselves. I'm sure it was not only to come up with names and reasons, but also to determine if Emma Jane would approve. That was all right. I had nowhere else to be and a keen sense my time was running short. It had been over forty-eight hours since Jonathan's murder. Not knowing how fast the wheels of justice turned in Crockett County, Texas, I needed to be prepared before my possible arrest.

My heart sank a bit as the other women left without saying another word. I truly thought I had piqued their interest. Denise waited for the door to close before she walked over to stand in front of me, her back to the window where the women were now peering through. "I need you to act disappointed in what I'm about to tell you."

She wasn't making sense, but I figured I had nothing to lose by playing along. I crossed my arms and stood stiffly, managed a small pout with my lips, and started shaking my head. "This work?"

Denise's grin gave me my answer. "The other women aren't willing to cooperate, but I really do like that goblet. I'll keep thinking about names and discreetly asking around, but the Bizzy bodies not only hated Jonathan, they hated the RV park he owned."

This was new information. I hadn't realized that Jonathan not only lived in the RV park but owned it as well. I also recalled Karen sharing with me about which house was theirs. I'm pretty sure it was the one with the high privacy fence around the property situated just across from the RV park. Very interesting. "Thank you," I mouthed, then followed it up with a verbal response loud enough for her friends to hear. "How disappointing. If you change your mind…"

Denise winked. "Just saved myself fifteen dollars. Looking forward to adding to my savings." She turned with a satisfied smirk, which worked for both me and her waiting sheep. Once they were no longer in visual range, I allowed myself a smile as well. Fifteen dollars was a small price to pay for what I'd learned.

Deciding to give Denise a little extra incentive, I placed a "Reserved" card in front of the goblet she'd been admiring. Didn't want anyone else purchasing her motivation. I could procure another similar one from my climate-controlled storage unit outside of town, but since business hadn't been exactly booming, there was no reason to be in a hurry.

The one and only young person I'd met in town, Emerson, came into the shop just before lunch. His dark hair resembled a mop on top of his head. I'm sure it gave him fits trying to tame it. Mine was the same during the humid summers. "Hi, Emerson."

"Hello, Ms. Sadie. I brought these for you." He extended a sprig of beautiful flowers made up of vivid colors. "My aunt wanted you to have them. She feels bad that not many people have been in your shop."

"That's very kind of her. Let me get a vase."

A few minutes later, I'd procured the item, filled it with the appropriate amount of water, and the flowers now brightened up the corner of the checkout area. "I'll have to stop by and say thank you to your aunt."

The look on his face was priceless, but he said nothing. I decided to let him off the hook since I suspected he was the one responsible for this sweet gesture. "You hungry?"

His shoulders shrugged. "I'm a teenage boy. I can always eat."

"I'll try to remember that for when I have nephews. I did promise you lunch, and I always keep my promises." I handed him the *Closed For Lunch* sign. "If you'll put this on the door, I'll grab the food."

I divided up the antipasto I'd brought for lunch, making sure Emerson had the bigger portion. He was a growing boy, after all. Grabbing silverware and two bottles of Acqua Panna mineral water, I carefully transported our meal to the front. When Emerson saw what was for lunch, his gaze brightened and he licked his lips. It pleased me that he was excited about the meal.

Before I could say anything further, he grabbed the fork and went to work on the food. I chuckled. "You weren't lying about being hungry."

He finished the bite in his mouth and offered me a bashful grin. "You always keep your promises, and I never lie."

"Never?"

His mop of black hair shook to confirm it. "No, ma'am. My parents always taught me the truth would set me free."

"They sound like wonderful people. I wish I could've known them." Of course, given the number of times I'd lied over the years to help my clients ensure the truth was revealed about the liars and cheats taking unfair advantage of them, his parents probably wouldn't have liked me.

Emerson didn't say anything in return but resumed eating. I decided to change the subject. "What do you want to be when you grow up?"

A slow smile emerged on his thin face. Whether that was due to the change of subject or the thought of what he wanted to be, I couldn't be sure. "Police chief here in Wilson."

I grinned. "You should think big. Why not president of a board, or mayor of Carson? Isn't that where the real power resides?"

"Maybe, but I'm not a fan of politics."

"How old are you again?" He'd told me, but everything that came out of his mouth was very mature for his age, so I needed to double check.

"Fourteen."

My curiosity spiked. "And why aren't you a fan of politics?"

His bashful grin warmed my heart. This kid truly was something special, even if I didn't have the whole story about him yet. "I listen and pay attention to everything that happens around me. Figuring people out is kind of my thing."

He and I had a lot in common. "Tell me more."

"No one pays much attention to a kid, especially a teenager who sits quietly in a corner reading a book I've learned to watch people's faces and how they act in different situations. People motivated by power will lie, cheat, and try to manipulate the people they supposedly are friends with."

At his tender age, I didn't want to share the unhappy news that most people would lie, cheat, and manipulate others to get what they wanted. "What about the ladies' association here in Wilson? Any chance you've had the opportunity to observe them?"

"My aunt is a card-carrying member, so I've overheard a lot of conversations. When I'm not in school, I help with the sound system at their monthly luncheons."

Guilt tugged at my heart strings. This kid was about the purest person, besides my mother, I'd had the privilege of meeting. I didn't want to lie to him, but I also needed information he might possess. I opted for the truth. "Then, I'm sure you know Emma Jane Birmingham."

He nodded. "She's the president of the ladies' association."

"I've learned over the last day or so that she wanted this storefront for a project. She's pretty upset at me for taking it away from her." I could've sugar-coated it, but this was the unvarnished truth. I'd known there was another potential lessor, so I'd sweetened the deal to ensure I'd get the lease rather than the other interested party.

"She likes to get her way."

That was an understatement, but I continued with a small smile. "Most adults do. Any chance you know what that pet project was?" Figured if I could find a way to help make that happen, we might not be friends, but maybe I wouldn't be number one on her hit list.

Emerson's eyes closed. I assumed he was thinking or trying to remember. Maybe he was repulsed by my asking so many questions. Either way, I would wait to see if he would share. After a few more moments, he opened his eyes. "She was going to open a consignment shop. The idea was the women would bring in their cast-offs to be sold. Five percent of the net proceeds were designated for the local shelter."

My face responded before I could control it. "That doesn't feel very charitable."

His giggle came out a mix between the squeaky notes of a teenager and the beginnings of a voice changing to a man's. It was adorable. "Not charitable at all."

"Thank you for telling me, Emerson. I appreciate you."

"Thank you for being honest with me."

"I promise to always try. Sometimes, the lies come easier for me than the truth." Wow, this kid was like a truth serum or something. Good thing I didn't know him before I moved here. He would've spelled disaster for me, my team, and my clients.

"I believe you. And I haven't forgotten."

Apparently, I had. "Forgotten what?"

"I'm still working on learning who else might have wanted Mr. Kirkpatrick dead."

Clearing our lunch dishes, I shared, "That list grows longer by the day. You probably know that I'm at the top of Chief Parker's list of suspects. You don't happen to know why they haven't arrested me yet, do you?"

"No, but Chief Parker and I are buds. I'll see if he will tell me anything. But don't get too hopeful. He's a by-the-book kind of guy."

"Fair enough. That could be why. He wants to make sure he has evidence and motive."

Emerson nodded, "That's probably it."

I laughed. "Have a great day, Emerson."

"You, too, Ms. Sadie."

The rest of the afternoon passed by uneventfully until right before closing time. When the door opened, my heart dropped to my knees. In walked Deputy Jake Matthews. This was it. My time was up. "Good afternoon, Deputy."

He removed his cowboy hat as he gazed around the roomful of treasures and nodded. "Ma'am."

"Are you here to arrest me?"

The swagger he wore like comfortable jeans showed in his smile. "Not yet, but you shouldn't get too comfortable. The chief is making sure he's got his pigs in a row."

Pigs in a row? Maybe that was a Texas expression I wasn't familiar with yet. Or maybe the deputy was easily confused. Either way, this was an opportunity to learn more and let him know I wouldn't be intimidated. "Interesting. I'm sure at least one of those pigs would be motive, right?" I decided sharing with him I knew he'd been bragging about having motive on me earlier would have just irritated him. As much fun as it might be, I needed to try to stay under his radar.

His face hardened at my statement. He took a few steps, which placed him dangerously close to my personal space. "If it were up to me, you'd already be behind bars. My gut tells me you're as guilty as they come."

I wanted to mimic his actions and take a step closer, but I didn't want to accidentally touch him and get arrested for a trumped up charge of aggravated assault of a police officer. I answered, "Then, I suppose it's good that not only is justice blind, but it's also not ruled by anyone's gut."

His skin flushed the color of someone who'd spent all day in the Texas sun without any sunscreen. "Enjoy your last day or two of freedom. Tick tock–time is running out." With his final warning, he turned and exited as quickly as he'd arrived.

On my way home, I tried to put the unpleasant encounter out of my head. If Chief Parker was as by-the-book as Emerson indicated, and I had no reason to believe otherwise, he was probably building his case. Which meant he was trying to poke around in my past. The decade or so I'd essentially been undercover and using aliases would certainly be giving him pause as, by official records, Sadie Sabatini had dropped off the face of the earth after she'd earned her associate degree in business. No rental records, no credit card receipts other than once a year for Christmas, and no digital footprint. I'd essentially been a ghost for ten years. No wonder Deputy "Pigs in a Row" was anxious, he wanted the arrest and to close the book on the two newcomers to town. One murdered, the other the murderer. Maybe he should just put up a sign: "New folks not welcome."

Shaking my head to dispel the gloom, I noticed signs had been put up promoting a local market with pop-up shops. The event was being held tomorrow afternoon to promote community businesses. One part of me railed against the injustice that my shop had not been included; the other figured Emma Jane was probably in charge, so this intentional slight was part of her master plan to ensure my business failed. I stopped long enough to grab a flyer from the little holder on one of the signs to ensure I had all the details. A plan was already formulating. I'd iron out the details later tonight, but now I had a date to get ready for. Might as well enjoy my potential last night of freedom with some Italian food someone else cooked.

Normally, choosing what I would wear was easy. Besides wanting to spend time with Jeremy, another goal for this evening was to get him to share information with me. The dress I held in front of me had been a favorite of mine when running the Sexy Blonde Con. Men had a distinct weakness for women dressed in a shimmery, provocative black dress. Even those who would never consider doing anything to betray their vows or cheat on their girlfriends couldn't help but be distracted. And when men were distracted, they tended to say things they normally wouldn't.

With a sigh, I returned the dress to the back of my closet. Another indicator Jeremy was different. I wanted him to share things with me because he wanted to, not because I tricked or distracted him. Settling on a black skirt with a black and white blouse with straps that criss-crossed around my neck and left my shoulders bare (hey, I wanted him to notice me), I hurried to finish getting ready. Being late wasn't an option, and neither was getting a ticket.

Francesca's turned out to be not only a restaurant that served Italian food, but it also looked like it had been transported directly from Tuscany. The walls were lined with shelves boasting wine bottles that matched the ambiance of the entire room. A curved brick ceiling and dark wood furniture reminded me so much of the stories my father shared about his travels throughout Italy.

"Hello, Sadie." Jeremy's deep voice prompted me out of my memories.

I turned toward the sound of his voice to find him standing there in dark slacks and a crisp white button-up, short-sleeved shirt that highlighted biceps which, along with the rest of his body that I could see, had been kissed perfectly by the sun. Words escaped me. He was magnificent.

"Sadie?"

Oh, yes, that was me. I blushed good-naturedly, thinking maybe he was running the Sexy Blonde Con on me. I was certainly distracted. Remembering Sadie Jenkins had a Southern accent, I responded. "Sorry. Hi, Jeremy."

He nodded but didn't boast the satisfied smirk I would've expected. "Our table is ready."

A small alarm triggered in my brain, but I couldn't determine for what reason. He truly was distracting. Maybe that was the alarm? I hadn't been properly distracted in decades, which could explain why I was unfamiliar with this warning.

After being seated and ordering drinks, wine for me and water for him, I decided to start the conversation. "Thank you for joining me. I confess I was a little surprised, but very happy you texted."

"I had a reason."

I learned forward and smiled. "Oh? And what might that be?"

He followed suit and leaned forward as well. His voice was low and barely above a whisper. "I did some digging. Your blog site is as fake as I suspect you are. Other than on the website you provided, there's no digital footprint for Sadie Jenkins."

And there you have it. The number one reason why I couldn't be emotionally involved with anyone. It also proved I shouldn't try to run a con without my team, at least not one that involved the digital world. Leaning back, I sighed and responded in my normal voice. "Guilty as charged, officer." I considered throwing in a tease about handcuffs, but decided it was best to cut my losses. I'd enjoy my wine and dinner solo and then focus on the matters that were most important—ensuring I didn't go to jail for a murder I didn't commit.

Deciding the truth, once again, would serve me best, I continued. "My real name is Sadie Sabatini. I recently moved to Wilson and opened a shop called Tesoro. You should stop by sometime. There are some beautiful pieces I'm certain your girlfriend would love." Okay, so I might have still been fishing for information. Though there was little to no chance he and I had a future, I still wanted to know more about him.

"Why did you lie?"

So, he wasn't going to offer up any information on his relationship status. Fair enough. I responded with a shrug. "I needed information, and I didn't think you'd tell me if I just asked."

"Why are you so curious about the death of Jonathan Kirkpatrick?"

If we were playing Truth Or Dare, I'd have chosen a dare without hesitation, but I knew Jeremy would not be amused. I gazed into those beautiful eyes and shared, "Because I'm Chief Parker's number one suspect. He hasn't arrested me yet, but I'm certain my time is running out."

"Did you kill him?"

His question was technically a yes or no, and I was certain he expected I would say no even if it wasn't the truth, so I opted for a different tactic. I leaned forward again. "What does your gut tell you?"

He stared at me long enough that I knew I could get lost forever. Before I could start naming our children, he shook his head and broke our connection with a sigh. "No. No, I don't think you did."

Relief washed over me and gave me hope that maybe all wasn't lost. I would much rather choose Jeremy's well-defined gut over the deputy's skinny one. "Thank you."

"For what?"

"For believing in my innocence. I didn't kill him, but I don't think they've looked any farther than me for suspects."

The waiter brought our drinks, and I took a long sip, hoping to ease the trauma of the day. While I enjoyed the wine, Jeremy ignored his water. "I bet you've been searching for alternate theories of the crime, haven't you?"

"You best believe it."

"Have you found any?"

At this point, what did I have to lose? I'd lied to him about who I was, so there wasn't any chance at being the future Mrs. Jeremy Raber, but I could use a few more friends. "Three so far, and I'm working on more."

The waiter appeared and we ordered. Once alone again, he resumed our conversation. "Who do you have?"

"Estelle Zimmerman. As far as I've learned, she was the last person to see him alive. She also had a romantic interest in him."

"Why would she kill him?"

I blushed. "He did try to kiss me."

Jeremy's laugh was rich and deep and caused a pleasant ripple effect in my stomach. "Must've been some kiss."

Deciding to play along, I offered a sly grin. "Wouldn't you like to know?"

This time, I noticed a faint pink hue on his tanned skin. Maybe I was still capable of being just a little distracting. "Even if it had been epic, it hardly justifies murder from a jealous lover."

Spoken like he'd watched a lot of *Law & Order*. To end any speculation on his part, I clarified, "It wasn't even a kiss, so I agree. Motive is thin with her, more of a means and opportunity that landed her in my possible suspects list."

"Fair enough. Who else?"

"Pete Jensen. He and Jonathan were negotiating over a piece of land, but it wasn't progressing to Pete's liking. He has a temper and his exact whereabouts the night of the murder are unknown."

"You haven't confirmed his alibi yet?"

I shook my head, ashamed that I hadn't been able to find a way to do so. "I've been in town less than a month.

According to Pete's wife, he was at a poker game at Ted and Emma Jane Birmingham's house. I'm not on Emma Jane's list of favorite people, so I haven't asked because she would either lie or tell me to pound sand."

"Can't hurt to try, especially if time is running out."

An exasperated sound escaped my lips, "Fine. I'm sure I'll see her tomorrow at the little marketplace I wasn't invited to but have decided to go to, anyway. It's not like me to not at least try."

"That's the spirit."

Our food arrived and we spent a few minutes simply eating and enjoying the wonderful cuisine. "This is magnificent. Thank you for recommending it."

"I figured you'd appreciate it more than most."

"You figured Sadie Jenkins would appreciate Italian cuisine?"

His chuckle sounded as sexy as his laugh. "Your fake last name aside, I could tell from looking at you there was Italian heritage in there."

Flirty responses flew to the tip of my tongue, but I figured this was a one-time deal so I simply said, "You're very observant. Thank you."

The smile on his face looked genuine to me. If he was faking it, he was good. Very good. He didn't strike me as anything less than exactly who he portrayed, a *what you see is what you get* kind of guy. I, on the other hand, was pretty much the polar opposite. Of course, they say opposites attract...whoever "they" are. But I'd chosen to start a relationship with a lie, so this was about as good as it was going to get.

Normally, I would ask him about his job, childhood, and other personal matters. Since I wasn't prepared to answer any questions in return, I kept it professional. "A woman I met in Wilson mentioned that both the EPA and the game warden were keeping an eye on Lester Price. He's also on my list of possible suspects. I witnessed a heated exchange where Lester threatened Jonathan. Any insight?"

Jeremy took another bite of his food and a drink of his water before answering. My guess was he was trying to determine how much, if anything, he was going to tell me. "My gut tells me he's dirtier than the bottom of Lake Amore, but I've not been able to prove it."

"Is he capable of murder?"

There was a long pause. For what reason, I had no idea. This was pretty much a yes or no kind of answer. Finally, he spoke. "I don't want to believe anyone is capable of murder, but I know that's not reality. If Mr. Kirkpatrick had found something on Lester that I missed, he might have killed him to protect his secret."

His words both warmed my heart and iced it. Warmed it because I loved his view of the human spirit and the belief he held that there was inherent good in people. Though, I knew without a doubt that wasn't true. People were calculating and would do anything to protect that which they loved, whether it was people or material possessions. The ice in my heart was from the realization that if having dirt on Lester was the only reason he might have to murder Jonathan, then there was no reason at all. Jonathan had confessed to me in our brief time together that he hadn't been able to find anything yet. "I love that you believe that. Sadly, I've seen people hurt or kill others for far less."

He reached across the table and laid his hand over mine in a comforting gesture. "I'm sorry that's your view of life. You must have seen some terrible things over the years."

Though he had no idea, truly, what my life had been or what I'd seen, this was probably an opening for me to share more about myself. I'm sure curiosity was the reason. I know I had at least a million questions I wanted to ask him about his life but, once again, I avoided getting personal. "Jonathan shared with me that he still didn't have anything concrete on Lester, so if that's the only reason you can think of for murder, he's a dead end."

His hand withdrew, the tender moment over. I'd essentially poured a glass of Italian sparkling water over whatever small ember for our future might have remained. He picked up his fork to resume eating. "I know some attorneys that might be helpful, should the need arise."

"Thank you. I appreciate the offer." I paused for a few moments, finding my courage. "Does that mean you'll take my call?"

His face disappeared as his large, capable hands covered his beautiful eyes. He rubbed at them for a moment before lowering his hands and gazing directly at me. "I want to be honest with you and say I don't think there's a future for you and me. We're too different, and you're a closed book to sharing anything about yourself, really."

"I know."

"I can't be in a personal relationship with someone I don't know and, I'm sorry, can't trust."

"I understand." It saddened me beyond words, but I knew until my life was in such a place I felt safe to share about it with someone, this soundbite was going to be on repeat.

"But despite all of that, I would still take your call." He ended his statement with a small smile.

He'd offered me a thread. A small thread that I could maybe someday add to and make stronger. I nodded. "Thank you for that. I appreciate it. I hope I can eventually earn even a little more of your trust."

"Me, too."

The server arrived. "Dessert?"

I looked to Jeremy to see if he wanted any, but he shook his head. "Just the check, please."

The server laid the small tray with the piece of paper on the table in front of Jeremy. I quickly snatched it away.

"Hey!" Jeremy's face heated as one hand went to the back of his neck and began to rub it in a soothing gesture. The look he shot me said more than any words could at that moment.

I smiled at the server and then directed my explanation to Jeremy "I promised to treat you to dinner. I'm keeping that promise."

He nodded, though he didn't look happy about it. Geez, did this guy want an honest woman or not? I pulled the cash from my purse, enough to cover the bill and a nice tip, and handed it to the server. "The change is yours. Thank you for a wonderful meal and service."

Once alone again, I returned my attention to Jeremy. "Thank you for letting me keep my promise to you. I know it wasn't much, but it was important to me."

"They might take away my gentleman card."

His Southern-tinted statement made me laugh I let my gaze drift over the fine male specimen that he was without letting it shift into a leer. "No one would ever take it away. And any person that spent even two minutes with you would know you are a gentleman through and through. Your status is safe."

He rose from his chair with a smile and offered me a hand to help me up. Though I didn't need it, I accepted it with grace. "Thank you for keeping your promise and for dropping the Southern accent. I like the Midwestern one better, anyway."

"An Italian-looking woman from the Midwest, what a puzzle I must make for you," I teased.

He gestured toward the door and allowed me to go first. "Maybe I like a good puzzle."

My heart responded to the little bit of hope he'd just added to our small thread, but I held myself in check. This was going to be a slow-play kind of deal. Assuming I found a way to move out of the number one suspect spot in the murder investigation, I had nothing but time.

Chapter Eight

It took me forever to get ready this morning, but appearances often were important. Crisp white capris, fresh from the dry cleaners, were paired with an aquamarine blouse accented with silver (which also matched my strappy sandals) and completed with handcrafted Murano jewelry. I wanted people to notice me and, most importantly, the jewelry. They were conversation starters and would draw people to my shop. At least, that was the plan.

Armed with my confidence and plenty of business cards, I headed to the club where the market was being held. I needed business, and I could use a few more suspects. The parking lot was lined with tables adorned with items from the local stores. I started with the first table, Tessa's Treats. I extended my hand in greeting. "Hello. I'm Sadie Sabatini, owner of Tesoro here in Wilson."

Thankfully, she took my hand and shook it. Southern manners always prevailed. "I'm Tessa Tucker. Nice to meet you. Please help yourself to a sample."

While I really wanted to try one of the Italian cakes, it felt too cliché. Instead, I picked up a delicious looking bar.

The crust was chewy, and the top half consisted of what could only be described as decadent sweetness. "This is amazing. What is it?"

"Texas gold bars," she shared as her stance straightened and a gleam appeared in her hazel eyes.

I noticed some wrapped individually in packages. "I'll take three. I'd like a dozen, but I don't want to be found in a dessert coma later today."

She laughed and we made the exchange. I also handed her a business card. "Fifteen percent discount for all the local vendors. I hope you'll give me a chance and come by."

I noticed her eyeing my bracelet. I moved my wrist closer for her inspection. "There's a whole section in the shop with items as beautiful as this one."

"I'll try to stop by." She took the card. "Thank you."

This action was repeated at each table until I reached Wilson's Floral Shop. I extended my hand. "You must be Emerson's aunt. I'm Sadie Sabatini."

She cast a quick glance around. I wasn't sure who she was worried about seeing her with me, but satisfied she could get away with being pleasant, she took my hand. "Nice to finally meet you, Ms. Sabatini. I'm Isabella Bailey. Emerson has told me all about you. I'm sorry I haven't been by to say hello yet."

I waved her apology aside. "Please, call me Sadie. No apology necessary. Emerson told me how busy your shop has been." I took a moment to look at all the beautiful arrangements she had on display.

Before I could compliment her, Emerson came running up. "Hi, Ms. Sadie. Glad you could make it!"

"Me, too. I'm grateful to have seen the signs yesterday to let me know this was happening today." While Emerson might not have picked up on my implied message, one look at Isabella and I knew she'd received it loud and clear.

"Emerson, can you go to the van and bring me a few more of the purple flowers, please?"

Resistance was displayed clearly on Emerson's entire body, but he answered, "Yes ma'am."

Wanting a chance to speak with him, I jumped in. "I'll walk with you. I could use one of those frozen lemonades. It's only early June, but already the good Lord has turned up the heat in Texas."

"Awesome. Be back in a minute, Auntie."

As we walked away, Emerson offered, "Thanks for coming with me. The only reason I didn't want to go is because we were visiting."

"Of course. I enjoy spending time with you."

He stopped walking and turned toward me. "I can't find anything out on Lester. I'm sorry. I've been trying but he only talks to his sister. She's nice but doesn't have much time to sit and visit with me. She runs the store at the marina. This is a busy time of year."

I patted him on the shoulder. "It's okay. I wasn't comfortable with you hanging around Lester, anyway. I might not be able to prove it, but everything inside of me tells me he's a bad man."

"Your spidey senses are tingling."

"My what?" I asked with a laugh.

"Don't tell me you've never watched any of the Spider-Man movies."

"Okay, I won't tell you."

He shook his head. "We'll talk more about that later. For now, I wanted to share with you what I did learn."

"I'm all ears."

"I checked with a friend of mine who is on the board for

the community here in Wilson. I asked what would happen to the RV park now that Mr. Kirkpatrick was deceased."

Apparently, this kid did know everyone and lots of things. I'd just learned about Jonathan owning the RV park myself. "And what did your source say?"

"She said that an attorney was due in town tomorrow to start settling his affairs."

This was not surprising, but I sensed there was more. At least, I hoped there was. "And?"

"She told me that Richard and Karen Bizzy had been in their office every day demanding they evict the tenants of the RV park and rid the community of the eyesore." He'd shared the last bit in a hushed whisper and added air quotes for emphasis.

This was news. "Is that what they're going to do?"

He shrugged his shoulders. "She said until the will was read and they knew how the property was going to be handled, they would all just have to wait and see."

"Any idea why Karen and Richard hate the RV park so much? They can't even see it from their house. That privacy wall keeps them from seeing out." *And anyone else from seeing in.*

"Property value, I'm sure. They talk a lot about that in meetings as well."

"You go to the CIA board meetings?"

"Of course." His adorable face scrunched up like there was no reason not to. My guess was that less than five percent of homeowners showed up at those meetings. I'd need to find out when the next one was. Needed to acquaint myself more with the people in power.

"Thanks for that information. Pick an Italian meal you want for lunch one day and I'll bring it for us to share."

"Cool!"

We got the flowers and stopped for a cool treat before returning to his aunt's table. He handed her the flowers and an iced lemonade. "Here you go, Auntie."

She placed the flowers on the table where they would accent the other colors best and then took a sip. "Thank you, Emerson. And thank you, Ms. Sadie."

The sound of heels on the sidewalk caused me to turn as Emma Jane Birmingham walked up to the table. Though the heat had climbed to the mid-eighties, she looked cool as a cucumber in her pale green summer suit. I'm certain I sported a healthy glow thanks to the walk with Emerson and the rising temperature. Deciding to see if she really was a Southern lady, I extended my non-lemonade-holding hand and smiled. "Nice to see you again, Emma Jane."

There was a moment's hesitation, but she returned the gesture. "I'm surprised to see you here, Ms. Sabatini."

I moved my hand to my chest and let a small gasp escape. It was overkill, I know, but it felt right. "Is this not a community event? Last time I checked, I was still a part of the community."

There was a small giggle heard from behind me. Emerson was enjoying listening to our conversation. Figuring I'd put a little icing on top of my minor victory cake, I added a little louder so those within earshot could hear, "As a new part of this community, I've decided I want to give back. I'm going to donate twenty-five percent of my net proceeds to the local shelter. That's a good cause, wouldn't you agree, Ms. Birmingham?"

How I managed to keep the smile off my face as my words registered with her escaped me. Perhaps, it was because this had been a spur of the moment decision, but it sincerely seemed like the right thing to do. Plus, Emma Jane had to agree since she was going to do it as well and everyone knew it.

She drew herself to her full height and offered a smile that didn't look agreeable or contrite to me in the least. "Of course. Giving back is always a good thing." She offered a deep, dramatic sigh (for maximum effect, I'm sure). "I just hope you're around long enough to make good on that pledge. I've heard you might have found yourself in a bit of trouble."

Emma Jane was baiting me, but this fish had learned not to bite. My response was limited to a shrug of my shoulders and a sassy smile. "I'm not certain what trouble you might be referring to, but I assure you that the truth..." I turned to Emerson. "What is it you told me about the truth?"

He grinned. "It will set you free."

Nodding, I returned my attention to Emma Jane. "And since the truth is that I didn't do anything to worry about, I know I'll remain free."

To her credit, she didn't back down. Instead, she lifted her hand to inspect her manicure and sighed. "We shall see, won't we?"

With that proclamation, she turned to Isabella. "I'll see you next Friday at the luncheon, right?"

Isabella nodded. "I'll be there."

"Good day, then."

With that, Emma Jane walked away. I returned my attention to Emerson and Isabella. Emerson was still grinning, but Isabella was not. "You shouldn't have poked the bear," she warned.

"Felt more like a bully attack from her than me poking."

Conflict flitted across her features. I felt bad putting her in such a difficult place, so I added, "I'm sorry my words to her made you uncomfortable. That wasn't my intention."

"Are you really going to give twenty-five percent to the local shelter?" Isabella asked with sincerity.

"Absolutely. Of course, that's provided the truth really does keep me free." Though I hadn't shown it to her, Emma Jane's comments had affected me.

"Sometimes the truth is hard to find, isn't it, Emerson?" Isabella returned to arranging her flowers.

He nodded. "Yes, ma'am." He looked at me, those chocolate drop eyes piercing into my very heart. "We've been searching for the truth about what happened to my parents for a long time, but still no answers."

Before we could continue the discussion, a well-dressed man came over. He appeared to be in his early sixties, slightly thick in the middle with salt and pepper hair. All in all, a nice-looking man who exuded affluence and power. "Good afternoon, ladies. Emerson."

"Good afternoon, Mr. Birmingham," Emerson answered. He was probably trying to help me out with a name, but the last name Birmingham didn't narrow it down enough for me in the town of Wilson.

Smiling, I asked, "Good afternoon, sir, and may I ask which Mr. Birmingham you might be?"

He chuckled. "I suppose that could be a little confusing for the new folks in town. I'm Ted Birmingham, president of the First Bank of Texas in Carson, and I serve here on the Wilson community board."

And married to Emma Jane. He'd left out that detail. My research into Wilson before I moved involved a lot of study of this influential and powerful family. Besides Ted and Emma Jane, the community also included Ted's parents, Robert and Dora Lee. There was also mention of Robert's brother, but not a lot of information on him. I'd surmised that particular Birmingham must have been the proverbial black sheep of the family.

"Nice to meet you, Ted. I'm Sadie Sabatini, though I'm sure you knew that already."

He laughed. "The grapevine here is strong."

Or his wife had shared plenty of her thoughts about me with him over a vast dining room table. "Indeed, it is. You should stop by my shop, Tesoro, sometime. I have many beautiful decorative pieces and a very selective line of unique and stunning jewelry."

"Maybe I will. Thank you for the offer."

Before I could start questioning him further, Emerson jumped in. "I'm sorry about your friend, Mr. Ted. I know you two were kind of close."

Ted's demeanor sobered. "Thank you, Emerson. I don't know if you could characterize what Jonathan and I had as friendship, but I certainly felt for his plight and was trying to help him."

Yet another tidbit of news Emerson was tossing my way. The kid was good. I decided to play along. "While I'm certain the grapevine has distorted the story about my inter-action with Jonathan, for the brief time I knew him, it was obvious he was passionate about being a part of the commu-nity." That was mostly true.

"No doubt, he was passionate about many things. I'm only sorry I couldn't help him more."

"How were you helping him?" I wasn't sure he would answer, but you miss all the shots you don't take, right?

Ted chuckled and put his hand on my shoulder. "Nothing for you to worry about. Just business matters."

The condescension in his tone irritated me. I wasn't sure if it wasn't for me to worry about because I was a woman, or because I was new in town. Either way, it was high class snobbery and I wasn't having it.

Remembering the lesson about getting more flies with honey than vinegar, I switched lanes entirely. "Enough talk about business. The grapevine also shared with me through Pete Jensen that you host a weekly poker game that's the best in town." That was a lie, and I was certain Emerson would call me on it later, but sometimes one had to elaborate a bit to get what they needed. "Though it's simply terrible about it turning into a bit of a tussle this past week." Since I didn't believe Pete's lie about the lawn furniture fight, I wanted to see if maybe there was one at the poker game.

Confusion colored his already tanned face. "Ma'am? I assure you, our game is non-violent. Just a friendly game of cards with cigars and bourbon."

"No place for a lady," Isabella chimed in. "But you're more than welcome to join us for bridge, mahjong, or any other number of games played every week here in Wilson at the club."

While I might be interested in such games in about twenty or thirty years, this place was currently playing a game with my life. My primary focus was on winning that game. "Thank you, Isabella. I appreciate the invite, but poker is currently my game of choice."

Ted offered the obligatory politician's smile. "Isabella is right, no place for a refined lady such as yourself. Now, if y'all will excuse me, I need to finish making the rounds."

I sighed as he walked away. All my efforts to get at more truth had failed. Before I'd settled on the decision to head home and find a new strategy, I spotted Chief Parker standing under the shade of one of the big trees surrounding the property. I turned to Isabella and Emerson. "If you'll both excuse me for a minute."

"You'll come say goodbye before you leave, won't you?" Emerson's hopeful question left me no choice but to agree.

"Of course. I just want to say hello to Chief Parker."

Without giving either one of them a chance to dissuade me, I walked with purpose across the parking lot into the blissful shade. "Afternoon, Chief."

"Ms. Sabatini."

"You expecting this gathering to need police attention?"

"No, but it never hurts to be present."

That was true. Often a police presence was a proactive way to prevent issues from arising. Not wanting to waste time, I got straight to the point. "Why haven't you arrested me?"

He chuckled. "If you confess, that would save us all some time. As I recall, you didn't have much to say on the matter except to proclaim your innocence."

"I *am* innocent."

"So you keep saying."

He was certainly a man of few words. The only person I'd met who talked less was Richard Bizzy. "If you're so sure I'm guilty, I'll ask again. Why haven't you arrested me?"

"I'm waiting for all the official reports to come in. I'll build my case, then make the arrest."

Emerson had been right. A complete by-the-book kind of guy. I was sure prosecutors loved him. "Are you even looking into other possible suspects, or am I your one-and-done target?" Honestly, this waiting game was driving me mad. I continued without giving him an opportunity to respond. "While you're waiting around, I've been investigating. There were plenty of people in this town who had a much stronger motive than an unwanted advance." No need to mention the blackmail attempt. Some things were better left unsaid.

"If you want to talk about this, you're welcome to come to my office tomorrow morning at nine. I'll take a full statement."

"While I appreciate your generous offer, perhaps you could invite Pete Jensen, Estelle Zimmerman, or Lester Price for that talk? Meanwhile, I'll keep looking for other suspects."

"Ms. Sabatini, I'll thank you to watch your tone."

This was getting me nowhere except potentially arrested for harassing a police officer or some other misdemeanor. It frustrated me that I'd let him get under my skin. This was not how I wanted to be portrayed. I offered the best smile I could muster. "Have a good day."

My internal temperature had risen to a point where it matched the oven baking the parking lot of patrons. It was time for me to leave. Not wanting to add to my list of lies for the day, I stopped by Wilson's Floral table. "Thank you for your hospitality and the offer to join you for games here at the club, Isabella. I appreciate that. Also, thanks for letting Emerson hang out with me some. I'm sure that has cost you a little with your circle of friends."

Isabella smiled sadly. "They're good people, just give them time. They'll come around. Emerson is a good judge of character. If he says you're good people, that's enough for me."

My smile reemerged, despite everything that had happened. Emerson was a bright spot in this universe, and in Wilson. "Thank you. You're raising a wonderful young man. Please stop by the shop. Not because I want you to buy anything. I just think you might appreciate, like Emerson and I do, the beauty of the craftsmanship. I can see that's true in the precise way you care for your flowers and arrange them in the best possible way. I do the same thing with my pieces. I offer this from one fellow artisan to another."

Emerson smiled as his aunt answered, "I promise to stop by soon."

"You both have a great rest of your day. Emerson, I'll see you soon?"

"Yes, ma'am. You want me to walk you to your car?"

"Such a gentleman, but no thank you. Help your auntie finish things up here."

My truck was parked at the far end of the lot and backed in for an easy escape. Some things don't leave you even after you retire. Denise was waiting for me, partially hidden between the vehicles. "I have another name for you."

The defeated measure of hope inside me raised its head to look around cautiously. "I'm listening."

"Alan Knightly."

"The name sounds vaguely familiar, but I can't place him." I decided then and there to go back to my research and review everything again. In all my excitement about Tesoro, I'd apparently not done enough study on the neighborhood.

"Recent addition to the local board. Young guy, maybe mid-forties. He's eager and filled with ambition. I'm sure he wants to be mayor or more someday. A bit of a looker, if you ask me." She smiled.

"Why is he on your list?"

"Jonathan had an ally on the board–Ted Birmingham. Everything Jonathan wanted, Ted pushed for."

"Do you know why?"

Denise shrugged. "Figured there was some side deal

going on. A *you scratch my back, I scratch yours* kind of deal. Isn't greed usually the motive for most things?'

I nodded. "Greed or lust typically top out the reasons for bad behavior."

"I'll take lust any day over greed." She laughed.

Wanting to keep her on task, I prompted, "So, Alan wasn't having it?"

"He was not. There were several confrontations between Ted and Alan about one or more of Jonathan's objectives. I witnessed a heated exchange around a week ago between those two. I kind of liked watching Alan get all fired up." Her eyebrows waggled as she grinned.

The effort to not roll my eyes at the insinuation in her last statement required the last of my patience. "And you're just mentioning this now? Have you told the police?"

Based on the way she looked at me, I'd offended her. While I needed her as an ally, even if it was in secret, we needed to be on the same page with expectations. She crossed her arms and lifted her chin. "Hey, no need to go getting all uptight. I'd forgotten all about it. I enjoyed the show while it lasted and then moved on with my life. It wasn't until I started thinking about people who might have wanted Jonathan dead that I remembered."

I sighed, leaning back against my truck. "Fair enough. I'm sorry. It's been a difficult day. Thank you for the information."

"I'll keep thinking. Don't sell my goblet."

This made me smile. "I promise, it's safe. I've already put a reserved sign in front of it."

Having received the assurance she apparently needed, she nodded. "Later, Sadie."

"Later, Denise."

Once safely back at home, I decided it was late enough

for a glass of wine. I settled on the couch with my feet tucked under me and picked up the burner phone that had Jeremy's number in it. Before I could talk myself out of it, I dialed his number.

"Hello?"

"Hi, Jeremy. It's Sadie. Did I catch you at a bad time?"

"No, I was just relaxing out on my back porch. You?"

"Just got back from a local event that was anything but relaxing. Your day sounds better."

"Sorry." There was a bit of a pause before he continued. "Did you just call to tell me that?"

I couldn't admit I'd mainly wanted to hear his voice. That was not something a woman of my age shared openly. I figured since I had him on the phone, I'd ask a question, too. "Honestly? I'm pretty worked up with this murder thing hanging over my head. Of the many places I like to be, the land of limbo isn't one of them. I spoke with Chief Parker, who was no help, by the way. He gave me no indication that anyone else was even a suspect, yet he still hasn't arrested me. What's taking so long?"

He chuckled. "Are you *wanting* to be arrested?"

"Of course not. It's the not knowing what's going on that's driving me insane."

"Listen, keep in mind you're dealing with a small town and county. Since they don't get a lot of murders, they share a coroner with the surrounding smaller counties. They probably even called one in from Houston for a situation like this. Since there's no family to demand immediate justice or apply any pressure, the autopsy wouldn't have high priority. Sadly, it may depend on how many bodies they received during that time frame. It's only been two business days since he was found."

"Guess the wheels of justice turn slower in the south."

It had felt like a lifetime since the deputy first showed up at my house, but, in truth, it had only been three days ago. "How much longer do you think I have before they bring me in for a more serious conversation where I'm compelled to talk?"

He sighed. "A couple days on the low end, a week max."

Not great news, but it still gave me time. While the coroner might not work on the weekends, I had no problem doing so. "Thank you for sharing that with me."

"You want the number for that attorney now?"

"No, but if the need arises, you're going to be my first call."

He chuckled. "Don't use me for your one phone call. I can't afford bail. I'll get an alert through the system about an arrest being made in the county. That will be my signal to reach out to the attorney."

"You mean bail for a not guilty but still arrested woman isn't in your monthly budget?" It felt good to be able to banter with him, even under the circumstances.

"No, but something tells me if we are to be friends, I may need to add that line item or start an automatic savings account for the eventuality."

While he meant it as a tease, his statement sobered me. It served as a stark reminder that life around me could be dangerous. "Seriously, though, thank you. I appreciate the information. I do feel a little better now."

"Not sure how I did that, but you take care and hang in there."

"Enjoy the rest of your day." With that statement, I disconnected the call and slowly sipped my wine while figuring out my next step.

Not wanting to blow my parents off since I promised to call this weekend, I sent a quick text asking to move it to tomorrow night, citing I had important errands to run. My mother sent a sad face emoji back but agreed to the new day and time. I prayed my call to her wasn't from a jail cell. While my parents could afford bail, I didn't want to involve them.

If I did need to access a large amount of money, I'd have to take care of that myself. This would require a call to a former teammate who handled the more discreet side of my finances. She was the only other person I trusted with the money I'd hidden away for a rainy day. Since I hoped she was enjoying her retirement more than me right now, I didn't want to involve her unless absolutely necessary. I hoped it wouldn't be.

I decided a walk might help me clear my head and focus on a plan. Normally, my team and I would bounce ideas off each other for the best way to proceed when a situation hadn't gone as expected. Since that wasn't an option, I'd have to use the current team of me, myself, and I to get this one done.

My feet guided me to my route by the RV park. I decided to get a closer view. Before going into the area designated as unincorporated, I slowed to study the property I believed belonged to the Bizzys. The privacy fence was very high, almost too high, I would think, to be in compliance with the deed restrictions. *No Trespassing* signs were also posted along with warnings that the area was video monitored. The Bizzys had effectively isolated themselves from their neighbors or, more importantly, from the RV park across the street. As I'd seen no evidence the RV people were disruptive or difficult in any way, it saddened me that they were being judged solely based on where and how they chose to live.

I walked into the area designated for the RVs and

surveyed each space. The gravel road in the park essentially formed an oval, almost like a racetrack. Lots were reasonably sized and spaced to allow each occupant room for their vehicle, the RV itself, and some lawn furniture on a nice patch of grass. The spots were around and inside the track. Everything was clean and well kept.

The few people sitting out in the grassy area on this beautiful Sunday evening waved and smiled at me. Some even wished me a blessed day. I'd made it about halfway around the circle when a man grilling some meat waved. Deciding he looked friendly enough to ask some questions, I started with something simple. "What's for dinner?"

"Steak and grilled veggies." He lifted the lid to show me, and I inhaled deeply.

"Smells wonderful. Much better than the pasta I have planned for the evening meal."

He laughed. "You're welcome to join me and the missus, plenty to go around."

His offer warmed my heart and reaffirmed my belief in Southern hospitality. "That is so very kind of you. Maybe another time?"

"Anytime. You looking to visit anyone in particular here, or just curious to see the oddballs?"

Though spoken in a joking manner, my guess was more than one person had come to see what these people were all about. "I don't think you're oddballs at all. You have a beautiful view along with a home and community that works for you. I see nothing wrong or odd about that at all."

He closed the lid on his grill and walked over to me. "I think you might be the nicest person I've met outside of the folks here in my little part of the community." He extended his hand. "I'm Hank."

Shaking his hand, I added, "And I'm Sadie. Nice to meet you, Hank."

Since we were now friends, I asked, "I actually have met a couple others who live here. Is Estelle around?"

"Estelle?"

Remembering her nickname, I corrected myself. "EZ, I mean."

Hank nodded, "She left about thirty minutes ago. Don't know when she'll be back, though." He pointed to a black and gray fifth-wheel RV that, based on how it looked, told me EZ was making a good living at The Foxy Lady. Maybe I *should* check out some of the clubs in Houston to pick up extra cash.

"Okay, thank you. Maybe I'll just leave her a note."

"Sounds good. Have a nice evening, Sadie. Stay for the sunset, if you like. There are some chairs on the dock. Pretty darn good view, if you ask me."

"Thanks, I appreciate that. See you later, Hank."

I continued my walk and, to keep up with the pretense, stepped into the lot where EZ's RV was to leave the alleged note. While there, I peered in the window on the front door. I couldn't see much as the glass was frosted for privacy, which made sense. Maybe she'd invite me over for a BBQ someday. Ha! It was doubtful, even if she had helped rescue me.

Figuring I'd spent enough time, I peered back and noted Hank had gone inside. I also didn't see anyone else within viewing distance. A few RVs later, just across from the dock, was Jonathan's RV. At least, I assumed it was his since there were flowers carefully positioned all around the area. Flowers to honor his death—another sign of the care this part of the community had for each other. Cautiously tiptoeing through the tulips and other plants, I walked up to the front door. I couldn't see anything inside his place, either. Hesitating only a moment, I reached into my back pocket and retrieved a small case that I always had with me—my lock picking set. It had been a gift from one of my team members who had spent a great deal of time and patience teaching me the art of picking locks. It was frightening how many times that particular skill had been used over the years. Sometimes to get myself in somewhere I needed to be, or, most often, to get myself out of trouble.

This time, I needed to be in Jonathan's RV. Making quick work of the lock, I stepped inside and closed the door. I inhaled and exhaled slowly to calm my racing heart. Getting caught inside Jonathan's place would most certainly land me in a jail cell. This was not on my list of things to do...ever. Once the beating in my chest slowed enough for me to concentrate, I looked around. Everything was neat, tidy, and in order.

I crossed my arms and tucked my hands carefully against my body. Since I didn't have gloves with me, as breaking and entering truly hadn't been on my agenda for the day, I didn't want to leave any fingerprints for the police to find. A gray leather couch was on the right side, and a matching loveseat adorned the left. Accent pillows were placed at each end. It looked comfortable, but I dared not sit on it to test the theory. The kitchen table was surrounded by the same leather seating, and two placemats were set out. A sole plant housed in a decorative pot adorned the center of the white table. The kitchen area on the opposite side boasted a glass top stove and stainless-steel microwave, sink, and refrigerator. Every surface was pristine and, honestly, reminded me of what a showroom model might look like. Either Jonathan was a neat freak with a healthy dose of OCD, or he spent precious little time here.

Fearing my time was limited, I made my way toward the back of the living room and kitchen space to where I assumed the sleeping quarters would be. Truthfully, the last place I wanted to be was Jonathan's bedroom, but I needed to better understand the man that everyone hated. Well, everyone except Ted Birmingham.

The bed was made, but I could tell someone had slept there. Everything else again resembled the clean lines, lack of clutter and missing personal items you would expect to find in someone's inner sanctum. Even in my bedroom, there were pictures, figurines, and other items that shared a little about who I truly was along with the things and people who were most important to me.

In Jonathan's private space, however, there was only one picture on the nightstand. Reaching in my back pocket, I pulled out a handkerchief. It had been my nonno's (or grandfather's, as they say here in America) and was mono-grammed with his initials. My papá always kept it folded nicely on his dresser in a place of honor. I'd convinced him to let me take it with me when I moved out. A way to remind me of the stories and my heritage. It also came in handy when I wanted to touch something I shouldn't. Though I was certain neither my nonno or papá would approve, I determined they would like it less if I got arrested because I'd left fingerprints.

I picked up the picture with the handkerchief and studied it. It was old but had obviously been preserved and protected well. A dark haired, very young woman smiled as she held a young boy. It didn't take a rocket scientist to figure out this had to be Jonathan and his mother. The picture looked a little askew in the frame, and something inside of me told me I should fix it to restore the precision and order Jonathan loved so much.

Though it felt odd that the one item in his home which I believed would have been his most prized possession would be the one thing not quite right, compassion demanded I fix it. Figuring I'd wipe the fingerprints off after, I set the handkerchief down and went to work on the little staples on the back of the frame. They were bent down to hold everything in place, but fairly easy to lift. I removed the back piece of cardboard and a small slip of paper fell out. Reaching down to retrieve it, my ears registered a whooshing noise before something very solid connected with the back of my skull. My world went black.

Chapter Nine

Black, to gray, to a fuzzy myriad of colors filled my vision. I blinked slowly to assess both my condition and surroundings. After the pounding in my head subsided enough for me to focus, I noted I was still in Jonathan's RV. Most importantly, I appeared to be alone. A quick check of my watch led me to believe I'd been out for around fifteen minutes. The hit had been hard, but not enough to do any lasting damage. At least, I hoped not.

Sitting up took effort, but I managed. I looked around and noted everything seemed to be in order just as it had been before I took my unscheduled nap. The only difference was that the picture and note I hadn't had the opportunity to read were missing. Just to be sure, I managed to get to my feet and took a good look around. Because there was such an order to everything, it didn't take long to determine the picture and paper were the only things missing.

Although tempted to get some ice from the freezer to nurse the growing bump on the back of my head, it was time to head home. Thankfully, my handkerchief was still where I'd dropped it. I carefully wiped down any surfaces I might have touched and straightened the bed, making sure it was as close to where it had been before as possible.

On my way out, I also wiped down the doorknob, the door itself, and the handrail on the steps leading to the porch. One could never be too careful. Repeating my cautious steps through the flowers and plants—not an easy task to do in the fading light—I noticed one of the planters had a Wilson's Floral tag on it. A close inspection displayed no name on the card, but it made me wonder if Isabella had brought it or, more likely, Emerson. He was a thoughtful young man. Of course, I couldn't rule out someone else buying from there as it was the local shop, but it did make me wonder.

As I made my way to the park exit, I noticed a Toyota 4Runner parked in the driveway of EZ's lot. I didn't want to assume the worst, but the timing seemed too convenient depending on when she'd arrived home. Though, how she would have known I was in Jonathan's RV was a mystery. I'd walked there, so it wasn't like she saw a strange vehicle. I'd shut the door behind me and made little to no noise. It didn't add up. Someone, however, had the same idea and picked essentially the same time to check out his place. I'd just gotten there first. Since I'd apparently made the rookie mistake of not locking the door behind me, their entry had been far easier than mine. I sighed out loud. I really was losing my touch.

I was in no position to confront EZ tonight, so I started the walk home. The Bizzy fortress was lit up like the Fourth of July with spotlights, motion sensors, and, I'm sure, cameras to enable them to spy on their neighbors across the street. A disturbing thought entered my muddled brain. If any of those cameras had line of sight to Jonathan's home, it was possible they'd seen me enter. Either way, I needed to talk to them again. If they'd seen me enter, they would reach out to their friends at the police department. Heck, they may already be on their way. Or, even more disturbing, perhaps Richard or Karen had been the ones to follow me into the RV?

Ignoring my growing headache, I followed the fence bordering their property until I came to a gate. I buzzed the security box. A moment later, Richard's voice replied, "Yup."

Part of me hoped Karen wasn't home so I could try to get something besides his standard one-word response for everything. "Hi, Richard. It's Sadie Sabatini. Karen had mentioned that if I had any questions or needed anything, you both would be happy to help. If it's not too late, may I come in?"

"Yup."

The buzzer sounded, and the lock on the gate yielded. I pushed through the iron bars that formed the entrance and walked the short path to the front door. Karen was standing there waiting for me. "Well, hello, neighbor. I'm surprised to see you."

"You did say you'd be happy to help me with any questions I might have, right?"

She nodded and stepped back to allow me entrance. Her home boasted a beautiful open floor plan. Clean lines and a soft palette of blues and teals accented the gray walls. "Would you like some sweet tea?"

"No, thank you. Maybe a glass of ice water?" I stopped short of asking for ibuprofen or Tylenol.

Karen turned toward the kitchen island where Richard was seated. "Would you be a dear and get Sadie some ice water, please?"

"Yup."

Even though it made my head hurt more, I chuckled. "He's a man of few words." More like one, but niceness over accuracy held more importance in this moment.

Karen shrugged. "He's not much of a talker. I'm good with that."

"Me, too," I quickly added, not wanting to offend her. At least, not intentionally before I asked a few questions.

Richard handed me the ice water. "Thank you."

"Yup."

Karen waited while I took a few sips, then asked, "What can I help you with?"

Not wanting to start immediately with her obvious dislike for the RV park, I opted for a more indirect route. "What do you know about Alan Knightly?"

Her brows furrowed as she leaned against the wall, scrunching her forehead into small little lines. Her gaze appeared far away. After a few moments, she straightened up, smiled, and stepped a little closer. "He serves on the community board. Not a fan of the Birminghams, and they're not a fan of his."

"Why? Ted seems like a nice guy."

"Ted's father, Robert, doesn't like the Knightly family. A feud that goes way back before Richard and I arrived in Wilson."

"Do you have any idea what started it?"

She shook her head. "And I don't expect it to end anytime soon. Between Ted and Alan butting heads at every board meeting and on every issue, to Alan's fascination with Emma Jane, the fire is fueled regularly."

This was news. I knew they butted heads because of Jonathan, but I'd had no idea Ms. Emma Jane was a source of contention as well. "Does Alan act inappropriately toward Emma Jane?"

Karen laughed, waving off my question. "He never initiates it."

The pounding of the bass drum in my skull kept logic from forming. "Then what?"

She leaned in closer. "Well..." Her voice resonated with a conspiratorial whisper. "The potential trouble it could cause doesn't stop Emma Jane from being inappropriate toward Alan."

Miss Perfect had some smudges, after all. Interesting. "She and Ted aren't happily married?"

"No, but from what I understand, they never really have been. Emma Jane is very protective, but I think that's more of the family name rather than Ted."

Her personality alone would be enough to turn me off, but some people were into that, I guessed. "Thank you for clearing that up. The information I had suggested it might be more of Ted's relationship with Jonathan that caused the rift between the two board members rather than Emma Jane."

"Oh, I'm sure it didn't help. For the life of me, I couldn't figure out why Ted had such a soft spot for that weasel, Jonathan."

Here was the opening I'd been waiting for. "Not a fan of Jonathan's?"

She huffed. "No, and don't pretend you were, either. You might have played it up at the club for whatever reasons you had, but word on the street is not only did you have a public and physical altercation with him, but you're the prime suspect for his murder."

Irritation over EZ's failure to share the truth, the whole truth, and nothing but the truth resurfaced. Time to get my side of the story out there...again. "My emphatic rejection of his romantic overture is hardly cause for me to kill him. The gossip mill is churning a little too hard on this one, don't you think?"

"Things are rarely what they seem. There's always more to a story, I've learned."

She was one hundred percent correct. There was more to my story with Jonathan. She, however, was not going to be privy to those details. "Based on the size of your privacy fence, I'd say you had a problem with Jonathan and the community he created across the street from you."

"Hey!' Richard piped up from the kitchen. Still one word, but it communicated volumes. At least I'd managed to get him to say a different word.

Exhaling slowly, I tried to de-escalate the situation. "No offense intended. Just confirming your theory that there is always more than one way to look at a situation. Besides being your neighbor, did you have any problems with him?"

"He doesn't...didn't belong here. That was obvious from the first time I met him."

"And the last time you saw him?" This was a total fishing expedition, but I had to put a line in the water if I was going to catch anything.

"At the club Wednesday night, before you sashayed out of there with your arm draped around him. No wonder he thought you might want a kiss."

Our conversation now resembled that of two high school girls rather than grown women. Time to make my exit. "Since there are apparently no witnesses to whomever interacted with Jonathan after our little tête-à-tête, I'll have to take your word for it. But know this..." I stepped closer and lowered my voice. "Someone else *did* meet with Jonathan after I was there. I didn't kill him. If I hear you spreading any information to the contrary, you'll learn quickly that I'm not originally from the south and my actions will effectively demonstrate that detail."

To her credit, she didn't make any outward acknowledgement of my subtle–or perhaps not so subtle–threat. Her dark eyes registered the truth in my words, however. "Perhaps, it's time you leave. Don't you think, Richard?"

"Yup."

And with that agreement, I exited the door and began to process the new information. The RV park's gentle hum of conversation called to me with its siren song of invitation. Since my head was hurting anyway, I might as well have that needed confrontation with EZ. I wanted to learn if and why she knocked me out and stole the picture. My feet took me in the direction of her home, but before I could make it five steps, my phone buzzed with an alarm. I retrieved it from my back pocket and opened the security app. There was an urgent message that the proximity sensor on the door leading to my garage had been activated. I clicked on it for more information, expecting to see the video feed. Instead, I got a pop-up note: *"Camera Not Installed."*

My aggravation level rose, which made my headache worse. Those cameras were next on the list to install, and my plan had been to do it this weekend since I'd been preoccupied with the opening of Tesoro. Of course, my weekend hadn't gone to plan, either, with the whole suspect cloud following me around. Casting one last glance at EZ's RV, I knew I had to save that conversation for another day.

While the temptation to run home was great, I'd promised myself I wouldn't run unless someone was chasing me...with a gun. A quick glance behind me confirmed I was on the street alone. Instead, I walked with great purpose in the direction of my house. I made it there in record time despite the accumulation of perspiration and continued pounding in my head. There might be something to this whole race-walk pace.

First, I inspected the door. There didn't appear to be any signs of a break-in, however, I reminded myself I'd picked the lock at Jonathan's and hopefully left no trace that I'd been there, so it was possible for someone else to do the same to me. Maybe I wasn't the only retired picklock in the community. Not wanting to contaminate any potential prints on the doorknob. I used another app on my phone to open the garage door. A fleeting thought crossed my mind that if I ever lost my phone, I'd be in a world of hurt. I made a mental note to create some back-up plans for that contingency, just in case.

Once the door was open, I performed a visual survey. I'd always operated under the premise that everything should have a place and that place should be consistent. It made it so much easier to determine if anything had been tampered with or stolen. Everything appeared to be in the same place, no evidence of anything being moved.

I exhaled slowly to release the tension holding me together. Maybe it had just been a curious deer looking in the door to see if there was any corn or other feed waiting for them? The cameras would be my first priority right after this whole Jonathan mess was cleared up. Sadly, I admitted to myself, that wasn't going to happen tonight.

I took some ibuprofen and waited for it to kick in. Once the bass drum in my brain quieted, I added some notes to my file:

Emma Jane has a thing (maybe) for Alan Knightly.
Alan Knightly opposed every Jonathan/Ted initiative in
Wilson.

Longtime family feud between Knightly and Birmingham family. No idea why.
Bizzys have "eyes" on RV park.
Could Bizzys have seen another altercation or motive for the murder?

The last thought I penned upset me. I should have asked more questions. They might not be as open with sharing now as they had been before. Well, at least Karen. Richard functioned barely above a mute. I would need to figure out another way to get the information or to get the Bizzys back on my good side.

A change of scenery was necessary to help focus my thoughts. An evening kayak ride sounded nice. The sun would be setting soon, so it was a perfect time to reunite with nature and restore calm to my soul.

A short time later, I was stroking efficiently through the calm water. Without conscious thought, my strokes took me to just outside the break wall of the marina. Slowly, I surveyed the structure of the docks, looking for any signs of defect or neglect. Something that Lester was doing–or not doing–at the marina had garnered Jonathan's attention. I'd seen the anger, perhaps even hatred, in Lester's eyes as Jonathan taunted him. That kind of visceral response, in my opinion, meant there wasn't a huge leap to murder. Yet, the police hadn't seemed all that interested in him. The chief didn't strike me as someone who would be on a criminal's payroll, but I supposed corruption could happen in a small town. I knew it happened in bigger towns and cities.

The temptation to call Jeremy and press him for more details loomed brightly on the fading horizon. He'd already admitted he was keeping his eye on Lester, but nothing had surfaced thus far. Maybe I could offer to help if I had more details.

I sighed, knowing that even with more information, it wouldn't move Lester further into the suspect spotlight. Jonathan had told me he hadn't found anything concrete yet, which I now knew meant something to blackmail him with. Maybe he'd just threatened blackmail? Even so, if Lester was running some kind of criminal enterprise—which already seemed a stretch based on what I'd seen—he wouldn't kill over the threat of blackmail. Only if Jonathan had the proverbial dirt on him would he have resorted to such extreme measures.

Knowing the answers weren't going to be found sitting here wishing I had more information, I stroked out toward the center of the lake to make my way back home. On the way, I noticed some other kayakers. One in particular caught my attention. This person wore a wide brimmed hat which shielded their face from the view of others. I supposed it also protected from the sinking sun, but would have been more appropriate for the afternoon brightness. Sensing my scrutiny, the person turned the kayak and began paddling away from me. I stared for a moment longer, appreciating the technique and power behind each stroke. I also noted he or she had the same carbon fiber, bent shaft paddle I had. Since those cost around five-hundred dollars, they either had to have more money than sense or truly enjoyed kayaking as much as I did for that kind of investment. Watching how effortlessly the person moved through the water, it was definitely the latter. Heck, they could have had a lot of money, too. It wasn't unusual for this area.

With nothing else to speculate on, I headed home. A protein smoothie and a salad provided dinner tonight. I'd indulged in too much pasta lately. A girl had to keep an eye on her figure, after all. Once I'd had enough to fill the void in my stomach, I dialed Jeremy's number again. This was becoming a habit.

"Hey, Sadie. You aren't in jail, are you?"

There was a tease in his voice, but it reflected my potential reality. "Did you get an alert?"

He laughed. "No, thankfully. Not about you, anyway."

This prompted my curiosity. "Well, maybe you can tell me about someone else's plight to keep my mind off my own?"

"Just a drunk and disorderly. You know I can't give you any names."

"Drinking too much and having some fun doesn't seem worth an arrest. Must be a slow weekend in Crockett County. Besides, it's not like I'm going to recognize the name." I paused. "Or would I?"

"Sadie..." Jeremy's tone warned I'd taken one step further than I should have.

"Okay, okay. I'll stop asking questions. If we're going to be the kind of friends you create a budget line item for bail money for, then you should know my curiosity is endless."

"I'll make a note of that. Thanks for the heads up." I was glad to hear the lightness had returned to his voice.

"Speaking of my curiosity, I don't suppose there's anything else you could tell me about Lester Price, is there?"

"Like what?"

"Like, if he's under the watchful eye of Jonathan Kirk-patrick, the EPA, and the county game warden's office, how has he not been fired?" The more I'd thought about it as I paddled my way home, the more I'd wondered.

A sigh was the response I received to my question. I wasn't sure if it was frustration with me or the situation he found himself in with Lester. "I've wondered the same thing myself."

"Have you been able to find anything on him?"

"Just code violations. Nothing super serious. He gets fined. It gets paid. He moves on with life. I continue to watch. It's very frustrating."

Even if Lester wasn't the killer, I really wanted to help Jeremy with this problem. "Do you think there's someone in the shadows paying the fines or smoothing things over with the board? They would be the ones to initiate actions to fire him, wouldn't they?"

"I've never lived in a place where there is a homeowner association, but I suppose that's plausible. If he had a friend on the board, it would at least explain him not getting fired. I don't know how much marina managers make, but I would think if they're making him pay the fines, it could become costly."

"Follow the money. That's what my father always says. If we can learn where his money is coming from, maybe we can figure out who is helping him cover up whatever it is they're hiding or doing illegally that you haven't found yet."

He sighed again. "I'll see what I can do, but resources are limited and investing that kind of time into a hunch may not go over well, even if my gut tells me there's something there."

I'd trust his well-carved abs any day of the week, but I kept that sentiment to myself. "I understand. Maybe once this whole murder thing has blown over, we can find a way to work on this together?" It was a thread I dangled, but I was hopeful he'd take it and add it to the one holding our friendship together.

"Sounds good. Get yourself out of the suspect spotlight and then we'll talk more about it."

I could work with that. "Thanks for taking my call, Jeremy."

"You're welcome, Sadie. Now, get some rest."

I disconnected the call but knew rest would not come easy. I grabbed my laptop and pulled up Google. Since this research wouldn't raise any eyebrows should someone look at the history later, I avoided the Incognito tab offered. I guess I'd done enough private searches that Google assumed that was all I was interested in.

I logged into my homeowner association page so I could access information not available to the general public. Clicking on the links, I finally arrived at the listing and bios for each board member: Ted Birmingham, Robert Birmingham, Delaney Jeffries, James Robert (JB) Nester, and Alan Knightly.

Color me surprised that there was at least one woman on the board—maybe progress hadn't taken a vacation here. I was more interested to learn that both Ted and Robert Birmingham served on the board. Nepotism was alive and well. No wonder Alan Knightly felt like he had to fight tooth and nail against the Birmingham family. It was two to one. I'd not yet met Delaney, JB—who I'm guessing was really Jim Bob in his childhood, hence the initials—or even Alan Knightly, for that matter. I'd only heard the rumors. Wanting to learn more, I clicked on their bios.

Delaney had lived in Wilson for a long time. Her husband, who was now deceased, sat on the board for many years. She had a degree in information technology and her background included contract work for many of the oil and gas companies in the area over the years. They had three children and she enjoyed charitable work as well as many of the local activities.

JB was newer to town, having lived here less than five

years. Truthfully, I was surprised he'd been elected. From what I'd learned about the process, it would be very challenging for someone who was relatively unknown to beat out a local resident with more tenure. Maybe there hadn't been any opposition? He worked for a company in Houston I didn't recognize, CellCo. A quick search revealed they had their fingers in many different industries, providing necessary products or chemicals to oil and gas, construction, and agriculture. I clicked on some information in fine print toward the bottom and learned they had entered into a new venture, both making and recycling the batteries used in electric vehicles. An interesting choice for a company with headquarters in the heart of oil and gas country. No wonder that was hidden as much as possible on their website.

There wasn't a lot on Alan Knightly. He was a handsome man, based on his picture. Dark brown hair with chocolate eyes and a nice smile. He was retired, though he didn't look old enough to me to be collecting social security. The bio didn't provide an age, so there was no way to confirm it. His face was thin and otherwise nicely proportioned. He'd been a resident of Wilson most of his life.

Next up was Facebook, another great source for information. You'd be surprised how much people shared of their lives for the whole world to see. Before I started my investigation on JB, I decided to see if Emma Jane had any public profile or pictures. I entered her name, and our own Emma Jane was front and center at the top of my search. The algorithms the search engines used could be very helpful at times.

All her posts were private, so I could only see the profile pictures. I expected it to be a loving photo of her and Ted together. Instead, the page offered a professionally done solo picture of her in all her elite glory. From the lift of her chin to the way she looked down on all those around her with those dark eyes that quickly discerned between friend and foe, Emma Jane exuded wealth and power. As was customary, her maiden name was in parentheses before her married name. Emma Jane (McIntyre) Birmingham.

Opening another tab on the browser, I entered her maiden name. After reading the bio, it was no wonder Emma Jane believed she was better than everyone else. She came from an incredibly wealthy family who had made their money generations ago with oil, gas, and a successful ranch with over a hundred thousand acres. I had no idea if that was average around here or not as everything was allegedly bigger in Texas. Either way, I was certain it provided them with a steady source of income and kept them in a lifestyle to which generations had become accustomed.

While I could have spent hours on Emma Jane, I needed to focus and get back to my imminent concerns, like proving Lester was as dirty as his beard. I entered JB's name. While some of the posts were private, a lot of the pictures were public. I scrolled until I recognized one of the other people in the photo. There, standing beside JB and his shiny red boat was none other than Lester Price.

Chapter Ten

Monday morning arrived without incident, but the alarm clock in my head began an incessant buzzing. My spidey senses, as Emerson called them, were on high alert. I needed to make progress on my investigation. My time had to be running short, even for a low-profile murder investigation.

Once Tesoro was open and everything was set for my customers, I reviewed my notes to see if anything revealed itself to me. Nothing. I picked up my phone and called Kelsey.

"Good morning, Sadie."

My heart warmed that she'd added me to her contacts already. "Morning, Kelsey. How was the rest of your weekend?"

"Decent. Pete has been doing his best to make up for fussing at me the other night."

"As he should. Has he mentioned any more about the property?"

"Just that he will have to wait for the attorney to arrive in town today to learn what the will says about the disposition of the property. Once he knows who the new owner is, he can then start working on him or her to cut a deal."

It made sense. Though, if Pete were the killer, wouldn't he have tried to learn who he would be dealing with next? If the person who received the property in the will was as stubborn as Jonathan, that could mean an equally difficult time to close the deal. As much as Pete irritated me at times, I had to believe that if he was the killer, he would have learned that detail before ridding himself of Jonathan. Otherwise, he was not an incredibly smart bad guy.

If the motive was even the property. Maybe it was something else? Kelsey had shared he liked to be close to Emma Jane. Maybe she was the key somehow? Though, for the life of me, I couldn't figure out how just yet. "I wish him luck as I know that will make him happy. And when he's happy..."

Kelsey laughed. "It certainly makes my life easier."

I didn't laugh, but my smile came through in my voice. "No doubt."

"Is there anything else I can help you with? I have an appointment with a customer at ten that I need to finish getting ready for."

"Oh, I'm sorry. Guess I assumed everyone was not as busy as me. Where do you work? I feel bad I haven't asked you that yet." I really did. I'd been so caught up in my own world and problems, I'd not asked any standard new friend questions.

"No worries, you've been preoccupied. I work at First Bank of Texas. I sell bank and investment services."

"Impressive! That's good to know. Maybe I'll need to open an account there and have you advise me on my investments."

"Anytime, my friend."

"Is Ted Birmingham a good boss?" I couldn't help it. I had to ask.

"Most days, yes. He's been cranky today."

"Oh? Any idea why?" Since she was the hub of the information wheel here in Wilson, there was no reason to suspect it was any different at work.

"Just rumors. His uncle is back in town. Arrived over the weekend." Her voice had dropped to a whisper, so I knew this was juicy gossip she was sharing.

"And?"

"And JJ is the black sheep of the family. While Robert did everything that was expected of him, including marrying Dora Lee, rising to power at the bank, and getting involved in local politics, JJ portrayed the picture of a spoiled and entitled rich kid. Rumor has it he left town when Ted was finishing high school or in his early years of college."

I wasn't certain why his nephew graduating high school would be a catalyst for him to leave town. There had to be more to the story. "Any idea why?"

"Like the Birminghams would make that public knowledge," she scoffed.

"Fair enough. If you think of anything more, let me know, okay?"

"Sure. Now, I gotta go. Stay out of trouble, at least until I get home," she warned with a chuckle.

"Have a good day. Thanks, Kelsey."

I pulled out my notes and added a few more details:

Robert Birmingham (Ted's father) has a brother, JJ.
JJ is the black sheep of the family. Left home when Ted
became an adult and went to college.
Robert married Dora Lee (as instructed?)

Ted married Emma Jane (not happy–always that way?)

I had no idea if any of that mattered. While the idea of arranged marriages weren't really a thing in the states, I was under no illusion that the pressure to marry the "right" person was very important, especially in families where generations of wealth and power had been carefully nurtured and protected.

My thoughts on the whole Birmingham empire were interrupted as customers started arriving at the shop. Perhaps, my appearance at the pop-up event on the weekend had made a positive impression. "Good morning, ladies. Welcome to Tesoro."

A couple hours later, the shop was empty and my sales were a little higher. I'd learned they were friends of Tessa Tucker, the woman who owned the sweets shop down the road. I would need to stop by and thank her for sending business my way. While there, maybe I could reduce her inventory of Texas gold bars. They were one of the best desserts I'd put in my mouth, but I'd never tell my mamma that!

Just before lunch, Emerson came in. "Hi, Ms. Sadie. How's business?"

"Hi, Emerson. Actually, it's been pretty good. Hanging out with you and your aunt over the weekend made me more respectable. Between that and Tessa's referrals, I've kept myself busy and out of trouble this morning."

"Ms. Tessa is good people. She makes the best treats ever!"

"Does that mean you're not hungry? I brought you some pasta with veggies."

He laughed. "I'm always hungry. Though, you could have left out the vegetables."

The way his nose wrinkled up at the thought of vegetables reminded me he really was a kid after all. "I know, but I want your auntie to know I'm taking good care of you when she lets you come visit."

"She already makes me eat vegetables with my dinner, but I'm sure she would agree with you." He sighed as he plopped down on the stool I'd provided.

"That's the spirit. Hold on while I grab your pasta and my yogurt." I laughed as his nose wrinkled further when I mentioned yogurt. It wasn't my favorite, either, but another one of those sacrifices a woman with a slowing metabolism made to keep her girlish figure, especially if more of Tessa's delights were in her immediate future.

After he'd finished half the pasta, I asked, "Have you ever met JJ Birmingham?"

"Only a couple of times, usually around the holidays. Ms. Dora Lee makes him help at the ladies' luncheons when he's in town. I think it's to keep an eye on him. He usually causes trouble when he's here."

"What kind of trouble?"

Emerson looked around as if to make sure no one would overhear what he was going to say. "Auntie says he likes to drink and carouse with the women."

The way he said *carouse* led me to believe he had no idea what the word meant. I smiled. "Sounds like the exact opposite of the image the Birminghams like to portray."

"What's it mean to carouse? I've been wanting to look it up, but since she only uses the word when Mr. JJ is in town, I always forget to do it later."

While I was certain Isabella meant to imply JJ had a way with the ladies, I knew it wasn't my place to have that kind of discussion with Emerson. He was very mature and, truthfully, probably already knew all about the birds and the bees, but I didn't want to be the one to reveal any new subjects to him. "Just means he likes to have a really good time." I narrowed my gaze so he could draw his own conclusions from what I said. I also stressed the word *really*.

Wanting to change the subject, I asked, "Speaking of really, I *really* enjoyed that Texas gold bar I had from Tessa's Treats the other day. What's your auntie's favorite choice?" I figured I'd continue to smooth the way with my fellow patrons by supporting Tessa's business and plying the others with sweets.

"White wine!" Emerson laughed.

"Oh, your auntie and I are going to get along just fine."

Before I could say anything more, my phone rang with an incoming video call. It was my father. For him to call me, especially in the middle of a day on a Monday...let's just say it either had to be bad or urgent news. "Emerson, will you excuse me?"

He jumped up from the stool. "I need to run, anyway. Thank you for lunch. I'll see if I can learn any more about JJ."

"Thank you! But be careful." I added the caution because if anything happened to him because of me...

"I'm always careful. Besides," he grinned and pointed to his face.

"I know. I know. Look at that face! Now, go be a teenager and have some fun."

A moment later, he was gone. I swiped up to answer my phone. "Papá, to what do I owe this pleasure?"

"Ciao, bella. I have information and figured if you asked me while on a call with your mother, it had to be important."

My father was very perceptive, and I loved him for it. "You know me too well."

His gaze narrowed. "Perhaps better than anyone." His implied meaning did not go unnoticed. I'd always suspected my father knew more of my clandestine activities than anyone else in my family.

"Perhaps. What did you learn?" Despite everything going on, it calmed me to see his face despite the worry lines on his forehead.

"First, promise me you aren't in any trouble." The concern in his voice gave me pause, making me second guess my immediate denial.

After exhaling a slow breath, I offered him a small smile. "Not yet, Papá. I promise you will be my first call should trouble find me. Right now, I'm trying to use knowledge to ensure I stay out of trouble."

He chuckled and shook his head. "My dear daughter, I know you. When trouble finds you, it's typically because you're trying to help someone. I can't fault your heart, but how you follow it leaves some room for discussion."

His words made my heart swell for the man who cared so deeply for his family. I knew he worried about me, more than I wanted him to, but that's what the best fathers did, right? "Perhaps, we can save that discussion for another time?" I smiled gently, wanting him to see through the small screen on my phone how much I appreciated him.

"As long as you promise I'll be your first call should that trouble find you someday."

"I promise." And I meant it.

"All right then, down to business." He put on his glasses and lowered his head to read the notes he'd taken. "Jonathan Kirkpatrick and his mother, Lydia, took up residence in North Dakota in 1984 when they purchased a modest home in a cash sale."

"Cash? She cleaned houses for a wealthy family. Even if

they were incredibly generous," which I doubted, "paying cash outright for a home takes some serious savings. Any idea where she worked once she got there, or where the money came from?"

My father smiled at my inquisition. My curiosity knew no limits, and he knew that. "The tax records show she was paid by an LLC. I have some calls out to a couple friends to see if I can learn any more about that. I'm sure it's a shell company of some sort. While I could probably find out with a lot of digging, I do still have a job that requires my attention," he teased.

"I know, Papá, and I appreciate you looking into this for me. I will owe you some big favors." With a smile, I continued. "Since I'm already indebted to you, any idea how Jonathan came into all his money? Did he receive a large payout from the same LLC his mother *worked* for?"

He shook his head. "Turns out their property had massive mineral and oil deposits below it. Jonathan sold the rights for an initial lump sum and a percentage of the monthly profits. Assuming the land continued to produce as expected, he would be set for life."

Processing this information, at least some pieces of the puzzle started to fall into place. Jonathan's wealth was new money. That explained why he had money but didn't really look the part. Something from his past made him want to seek revenge on the good people of Wilson, Texas. Logic would dictate that if his mother worked for the Birminghams and then abruptly left for some reason, they would be the people he would seek revenge against. What didn't make sense was that the one person in all of Wilson who had tried to help Jonathan was Ted Birmingham. Which made me wonder...

"Did any of the paperwork you ran across in your

research list who Jonathan's father was?" The timing could work depending on the ages of all involved, and would at least explain why Ted was helping him.

My father's gaze narrowed as he removed his glasses. "No, and having seen from the paperwork that Lydia worked for the Birmingham family before she arrived, I know where that mind of yours is going. People with that kind of money and power are dangerous, Sadie. Don't mess with them."

That ship had sailed, but I wasn't going to share that detail with my father. "I understand, Papá. Can you find out?"

He shook his head. "No, my little bird, I cannot. My circle of influence doesn't include those kinds of favors." He sighed. "However, in the United States, birth records are considered public records. If you know what county he was born in and a few other details which vary from state to state, you can request that information from the county courthouse."

Though I wasn't sure I had the kind of time necessary to make an official request, wait for it to be processed, and have the birth certificate sent to me, it was useful information for the future. Someone here in Wilson *had* to know, and if I could get them to tell me, it would save me precious time. "Thank you. I appreciate all your help. I owe you big time."

"Just call your mother soon and fill her in on this new man in your life." He pointed his finger at me with a smile. "You know how she worries about you and her future grandchildren."

Indeed, I did. "I promise to call soon with an update."

"I love you, Sadie."

"I love you, too, Papá. Give Mamma a hug for me."

"That I can do. Stay safe."

With that final instruction, he ended the video chat. After a few moments, I pulled up Wilson's website again and looked at the calendar of events. It took me a minute, but I found that the club was hosting an open bridge game for any ladies who wanted to participate. While I'd never played bridge, it would not be a stretch to show up under the pretense I wanted to learn. It would give me a chance to observe and ask more questions.

I made a stop by Tessa's Treats and saw there were more Texas gold bars available. While I still had some at home, I thought it couldn't hurt to show up at the bridge game with goodies. "Hi, Tessa. I wanted to stop by for a dozen more of those delicious gold bar desserts you introduced me to on Sunday."

Her countenance blushed under my praise. "Thank you. I'm so glad you enjoyed them. Are you sure you want a dozen? While I would enjoy the sale, I truly don't want you to end up in a sugar coma."

"I appreciate you looking after me. Someone should keep an eye on my sweet tooth. These aren't for me, technically. I'm taking them to a gathering."

The pale green of her gaze pierced me. "You're going to the club, aren't you?"

For some reason, I sensed there was some disappointment in that revelation. Whether it was because she couldn't go or she didn't want anyone else to go, I couldn't be sure. "I'd planned on it. I need some answers, and the people there could have them. A friendly face there with me would be nice. Any chance you want to come along?"

My answer relaxed her a bit. Again, I wasn't sure why. Her shoulder length brown hair would have swished with her head shaking if it hadn't been secured in a ponytail. "I appreciate the offer, but I'll pass. I tend to say whatever's on my mind, and that doesn't always go over well with that group." She offered me a wry smile. "Maybe one day I'll learn to behave like a proper lady, but not today."

I waved off her confession. "Proper is overrated, especially when it comes to being a lady. I've learned anyone can behave for an hour or two. Sometimes, you have to read the room and play nice in the sandbox to get what you want or need."

There was no way to tell if she'd received the life lesson I was trying to hand out for free, but sometimes wisdom had to soak in. Meanwhile, I needed her amazing goodies and then I'd be off to hopefully behave for an hour or so. I admired the way she'd carefully arranged and added a few garnishes to make everything look very nice. I paid her, adding a nice tip. "Thank you, Tessa." She handed me my receipt and my purchase all wrapped up on a nice serving tray. "Since you're headed straight to the club, I want my items to be part of the beautiful display of goods I'm sure will be there."

I lifted the plate. "Truly, this was very thoughtful. I think you're capable of doing anything you set your mind to, so stop worrying about everyone else and just keep living your dream."

My words had the right effect, if her big smile was any indication. "Thanks, Sadie. Good luck today and I hope you find your answers."

With a final nod, I was out the door and on my way. I noticed the closed sign was up at Wilson's Floral. Maybe Isabella played bridge? If so, that could make this a little more challenging. I wanted to behave and play nicely, but I desperately needed answers. Isabella might disapprove of my tactics. Regardless, it had to be done and I'd deal with any fallout after.

Once at the club, I was directed downstairs, where tables and chairs had been set up and women were already occupying most of them. I saw a table with some other items on it, so I placed the tray there and spoke at a level that would ensure everyone could hear me. "Since I'm new to the game, I brought some treats in the hopes y'all would let me watch and learn."

It only took a moment or two for several women to secure their share of the bounty. Kelsey made her way over to me. The smile never left her face as she leaned a little closer and asked in a hushed voice, "What's going on?"

"Can't a girl learn how to play bridge?"

She cut me a look that indicated she clearly didn't believe me but gestured with her hand. "Why don't you come watch our table?" Her voice lowered even further. "It offers players I believe you'll find of interest."

As we arrived at the table, I could see she'd just landed me in the proverbial pot of potential information gold. The table hosted eight. I immediately recognized Emma Jane and took secret delight in the face she was making upon my arrival. If I had to describe it, I would say she resembled an eight-year-old who had just been told to get out of the pool because of lightning. For some reason, her expression brought me great joy.

Before I could say anything, Kelsey jumped in. "Everyone, this is Sadie Sabatini. She owns Tesoro and is new in town. She's looking to learn to play bridge. Sadie, let me make introductions."

"That would be most helpful. Thank you, Kelsey." I was going to owe her big time for this. She was handling this like a trooper.

"I believe you know Emma Jane."

I nodded. "So good to see you again."

She lifted her hand in a hello but said nothing.

Kelsey continued. "Her partner is her mother-in-law, Dora Lee Birmingham."

Ah, the notable Dora Lee, current matriarch of the Birmingham family. I moved over to extend my hand. "A pleasure to meet you, ma'am. I've heard so much about you."

Her eyebrow raised and she blessed me with a half-smile. "And I you. Won't you sit so we can get back to our game?"

The question was asked with the sweetest of Southern accents, which made it hard to be contrary. I looked to Kelsey, and she quickly finished her introductions. "You've met Isabella and her partner is Delaney Jeffries."

None of the other names Kelsey shared meant anything specific, so I moved my chair so I was between and just behind Kelsey and Delaney. I watched for several minutes to try to get a feel for the game, but I knew it would require more concentration than I had to devote right now. I leaned forward to Delaney and offered in a hushed voice, "I was glad to see a woman served on the board. Your resume is impressive."

She kept her eyes forward and focused on the game, but a smile hinted at the corner of her lips. "You looked me up?"

"Of course. I'd love to have coffee or sweet tea, whatever the acceptable beverage is around here, with you sometime."

"I'm more of a liquor and mixer kind of gal."

Yes, she and I were going to get along just fine. And, truth be told, knowing someone who worked with computers was never a bad thing. "Oh, I knew we were going to get along famously. Tell me when and where. My treat."

Satisfied I'd created the beginning to at least one more friendship, I moved on to my main objective. "So, I'd love to hear more about how Emma Jane became part of the family. As your family is so well known and respected, I love hearing stories like this."

Emma Jane did not appear interested in answering my question. Dora Lee, however, beamed with pride. "We were so pleased when Teddy and Emma Jane started dating. His father had been pointing her out for quite some time, but it took several social gatherings and promptings before they realized what a perfect match they were."

Maybe there weren't arranged marriages, but this story felt like Prince Charming had no choice but to pursue his Cinderella. "So, not love at first sight, but maybe fifth sight?" I couldn't help but joke a bit.

Dora Lee waved off my observation. "No such thing as love at first anything. Love is born over time and with shared experiences and simply doing life together. Isn't that right, Emma Jane?"

There was no doubt in my mind the smile Emma Jane currently sported had been well honed in front of a mirror to achieve just the right touch. "Of course, Mother Birmingham."

"Her philanthropic efforts are to be esteemed, and her dedication to physical fitness and her health is second to none."

"I love to be out in the fresh air for my exercise. What activities do you enjoy, Emma Jane?" Maybe we could find some common ground, after all.

Emma Jane might have rolled her eyes, but I pretended

not to notice. She sighed, "I enjoy hiking, Pilates, and kayaking."

I brightened, maybe a few more watts than needed, but I was trying to make a good impression. "I love kayaking. We should go out together sometime."

"Oh, that would be wonderful, wouldn't it, Emma Jane?" Dora Lee exclaimed. "You could share with her all about your projects and other community-based agenda. She should definitely join us at the upcoming ladies' luncheon. Say you'll come, Ms. Sadie."

Though it was not my idea of a great way to spend a few hours in the afternoon, one didn't swat away an olive branch extended by the unspoken leader of this group of women. "Why, I'd love to join you."

"Perfect. Kelsey, you'll see to all the details?"

"Of course, ma'am."

"Can we please resume play? Some of us have matters to which we must attend this afternoon." Emma Jane's false façade was showing a few cracks.

I took mercy on her. "Of course. My apologies for interrupting your game."

"No worries at all, dear." Dora Lee picked up her cards and resumed the game, either uncaring or oblivious to the caged fury of her daughter-in-law.

When the first game ended, they made their way over to the table of desserts. I saw this as my chance to try to get some answers. I sought out Dora Lee, who was enjoying one of Tessa's gold bars. "They're delicious, aren't they?"

"Yes, just don't tell Emma Jane. She fusses about the processed sugar I consume."

I chuckled. "That explains why you're over here in the corner by yourself."

She raised one eyebrow but shrugged her shoulders and

went back to her treat. She probably was worried someone else would notice and tell Emma Jane. I found it endearing and humorous at the same time. Once I was satisfied she'd eaten enough of the sugar to hopefully make her more open to my questions, I jumped right in. "Please pardon my directness, but I'm feeling a little pressed for time."

Dora Lee stopped eating and fixed her gaze directly on me. "Directness in what?"

"I'm trying to piece some things together, and I fear only you may have the answers I need."

"I'm listening."

"Was Ted the father of Jonathan Kirkpatrick?" There, I ripped that Band-Aid right off. It wasn't the ideal approach, but desperation had begun to take up residence in my otherwise rational brain.

"I beg your pardon!" She directed an incredulous stare at me as her gaze blazed and narrowed. Her lips pressed together, most likely to refrain from telling me where I should go. And I was pretty sure it wasn't heaven.

I moved a little closer and lowered my voice, trying to de-escalate the situation. "No disrespect to your family is intended, and even if it is true, I'm not going to blab it to anyone. I'm simply trying to understand why Jonathan had it out for the fine folks of Wilson, yet Ted was so willing to help him."

She discarded her plate and crossed her arms. "I'm sure I have no idea what you're talking about."

"You are the matriarch of a very prominent family. There's no way you wouldn't know. Lydia skipped town when she was pregnant with Jonathan. Just using rough math and age guesses, Ted would have been graduating high school and getting ready to leave for college when she got pregnant. Maybe she wanted him to make an honest woman out of her, and he refused. Is that why she left?"

Her well-manicured index finger pointed directly at me as fire flickered in her cobalt blue stare. "You listen here, missy, and you listen good. Our family loved Lydia and considered her one of our own. We were devastated when she left. She gave no reason other than she needed to go. We had to accept that and move on with our lives. As far as Ted being the father, that's preposterous. He was and still is madly in love with Emma Jane. My son may be many things, but a cheater he is not."

Whether that was the truth she knew or the truth she wanted to believe, either way, it was her version of events, and no amount of prodding was going to get her to change her story. I knew I was going to regret my next question and I was asking it purely out of curiosity's sake as I didn't think it directly affected my case, but I was curious why he skipped town and never returned. "JJ left around the same time as Ted, I believe. I know you have watched out for your brother-in-law over the years. Maybe there was a reason besides you looking after the family reputation?"

A red flush crept up her sun-kissed body until she looked as though she'd spent entirely too much time in the Texas heat. "I'm certain you aren't implying what I think you are. JJ is a troubled man who has wasted away his portion of the family inheritance on women and wine. It's a miracle some angry husband hasn't put him out of his misery yet. Let me make myself perfectly clear..." She closed the distance between us, burning me with the heat of her rage. "You speak those words or make that inference out loud again and you will learn the dangers of messing with the Birmingham family. Do I make myself clear?"

I kept my tone level with hers to convey the urgency of

my position. "I understand your desire to protect your family. My only interest in asking about these possible secrets is trying to determine if they are affecting my life and future freedom. Otherwise, there would be no reason for me to mess with your family. I know you're upset with me right now, but I trust it won't always have to be that way." I truly didn't want to make enemies of the Birminghams, but desperate times and all.

"I trust it's time you take your leave."

Thankfully, the arrival of Kelsey saved me from having to say anything more. Which is good because I probably would have made things worse. "I need to get back to the bank. Sadie, will you walk me out?"

My gaze remained on Dora Lee. "I think it's time I leave, too. Dora Lee, again I offer my apologies and thank you for your time. I look forward to perhaps playing bridge with you again soon."

Her harrumph indicated she might not be as interested in that as I was. Without another word, she turned and left me there with Kelsey. I sighed, "I know I upset her. I wasn't sure how else to get the answers I need."

Kelsey just shook her head. "I know you're in a tough spot, but the old adage that you get more flies with honey rather than vinegar has some merit."

We both already had our purses, so I gestured toward the stairs. As we started the climb, I made an effort to explain. "I understand what you're saying, and I will try harder. Do you remember how you asked Pete about the property deal you'd discovered when you were straightening the papers?"

"Yes, of course."

"Did you know he'd get upset when you asked him?"

She sighed. "Yes, I assumed that would be the result."

"But you did it, anyway, right?"

We made it to the top of the stairs before she stopped and looked at me. "Yes. Yes, I did."

"Because you needed an answer..." I led her down the path I needed her to go.

She nodded. "Because I wanted the truth."

"I need the truth to set me free."

"Pete and I have been married for a while now. You barely know Dora Lee. That makes the scenario a little different."

She was right. I felt at a loss on how to proceed. "I understand what you're saying. I'm worried the police are going to be knocking down my door any minute, so I can't be as delicate as I would normally be. I need to know who killed Jonathan, so I won't be arrested." I took her hand. "And I need your help."

She sighed, then used our joined hands to pull me into a hug. "What do you need me to do?"

Chapter Eleven

Once outside, we stood next to Kelsey's car. "Do you have an open appointment this afternoon?"

"Yes." She narrowed her gaze. "I thought I was going to be playing more than one game of bridge, but my friend needed to be rescued before Dora Lee destroyed her."

While I knew I could handle someone like Dora Lee, it gave me good-vibe goosebumps that Kelsey would come to my defense and sacrifice her afternoon fun. "You are a wonderful friend, and I'm lucky to have met you. I have a way you can help me, and I can help you."

"I'm listening."

"Let's go to the bank. You can give me your next time slot this afternoon. I plan to make this area my forever home, so I want to support you and your bank by placing a sizable investment with you."

While I'd like to think the gleam in her eyes was from me confessing I wanted this to be my forever home, it was most likely my use of the word sizable. I had no problem with that at all. She was an investment banker, and she had to make a living, too.

"All right, but please don't ask any questions that will get me fired."

"I promise to protect you throughout this entire transaction. And while I know you don't have much basis for believing my ability to do that, please trust me when I tell you that I've been protecting people and looking out for their best interests my entire life. Sadly, you've just had the unfortunate viewpoint of only seeing me trying to protect myself since we met. I promise you, that's not usually my end game."

She lifted her chin in response. "I appreciate that, but know I'm also capable of taking care of myself."

"Understood." I pointed to her car, then to mine at the end of the lot. "I'll meet you there?"

"Sounds good. We'll say two-thirty for your appointment. That will give me time to get there, get settled, and add you to my schedule."

"Fair enough. Thank you, Kelsey." I pulled her into a quick hug before heading to my truck.

Since I had a few minutes, I swung by my house and did a quick change of clothes. While I looked perfectly fine for a ladies' bridge game, my goal here was to impress the males of the Birmingham family and get them talking. Hopefully Dora Lee was more invested in her bridge game than calling her husband or son to complain about me. Since I'd implicated both in reputation-ruining scenarios, I had to hope Dora Lee would keep that to herself to avoid it getting out into the universe. Maybe as she and Robert were snuggling in their king-sized bed and satin sheets tonight, she might tell him. By then, I would have already gotten the information I needed.

Hopefully.

The First Bank of Texas stood proudly in the afternoon

sun. The white of the exterior boasted architectural accents like triangles over the windows, a beautiful upscale white picket fence, and, of course, the gold Texas star predominantly displayed on the front of the building. Texas and American flags waved proudly in the slight breeze we'd been blessed with, keeping the temperatures right around a hundred. Given this was the heat index in early June, I wasn't sure I was looking forward to July.

The cool air welcomed me the moment I stepped inside the doors. The shiny wooden floors, matching oak and leather furniture, and more of the Texas star and flag rounded out the internal décor. Texas was a proud state and not ashamed to let everyone know. I kind of liked that about them.

"Right on time, I see." Kelsey emerged from one of the offices with her bright smile.

"I make it a habit to always be on time, even early, but I wanted to change first."

Kelsey gestured to her office. "You looked amazing beforehand, but I understand."

And I think she did. Once we were seated, she got down to business and conducted herself as a consummate professional who totally knew what she was talking about. I'd learned a lot about investments from my father over the years, so I made sure to ask all the right questions. I wanted to invest money with Kelsey, but I also needed to protect my nest egg. It was important she be the right person who would watch over the portion I entrusted her with.

We'd just finished up most of the meeting when I heard a door open and male voices filling the area. A quick glance confirmed it was Ted and another man whom I believed to be Robert. I worried that they'd concluded their business and Robert was leaving. I shot a quick glance at Kelsey. "Robert?" I whispered.

She nodded. "Let me get their attention."

Kelsey stood and moved to her door. "Excuse me, gentlemen?"

Being the southern gentlemen that they were, they couldn't resist a lady. "Good afternoon, ma'am." Robert offered a smile and dip of his head.

"Good afternoon, sir. Good to see you again. Might I trouble both of you for a moment? I have an investor who would like to speak with you."

The word *investor* got their attention. Ted made his way over to the door and saw me standing behind Kelsey. "Nice to see you again, Ms. Sabatini. I'm pleased you've chosen our bank to do business with."

"I'm very close to doing business with you. Kelsey has been nothing short of brilliant as she is reviewing all my options. You're very lucky to have someone so knowledgeable and connected within the community. She's the reason I'm here, but I'd like to have a word with both of you before I make my sizable investment." Yes, I totally threw in the *sizeable* again to keep their attention.

"Of course. Please join us in my office. We were just taking a quick break, but that can wait, can't it, father?"

"You know it can, son."

They followed me into Ted's office and shut the door behind me. Robert sat in Ted's seat behind the desk, which I found interesting. Ted took the chair next to mine on the other side of the desk. Leaning forward, Robert propped his elbows on the desk, his hands forming a steeple close to his face. "Now, how can we help you with confirming your decision to invest with us?"

I exhaled slowly. *Here goes nothing.* "First, thank you

for your time. I recognize how valuable it is. My time is limited as well, so I'll get straight to the point. As I'm sure you're aware, the rumor mill is always turning. Recently, I overheard what I'm sure is just gossip aimed at such a wonderful and prominent family, but you understand if I'm going to invest in your bank, that means I'm also investing in the leadership. I need to make sure these rumors aren't true before I do that, so I pray you'll forgive my directness." I said all of this with as much Southern charm as I could muster. Since my choice to outright come at Dora Lee hadn't worked, at least not how I wanted, it was important to adjust my approach this time.

Ted leaned in as well. I could see conflict on his face, though I wasn't sure why. He responded with a rush of words. "I'm certain a woman of your experience knows that the bank itself is protected from any of its employees' personal proclivities or problems they may have. Most businesses are structured that way."

Robert quickly turned his head enough to lob a few non-verbal arrows in Ted's direction. He then adjusted his demeanor to be all smiles and comforting as he returned his attention to me. "Of course, we understand there are always people out there wanting to tear down what we've built over generations of hard work and being smart. Ask your questions, young lady."

He'd already learned the same lesson Kelsey had been trying to teach me about the flies, honey, and vinegar. He was laying it on thick with the *young lady* comment, but, hey, I'd take any compliment I could get. I flashed him one of my award-winning smiles. No, seriously, I'd entered a contest one time as part of a con my team and I were working to get behind the scenes of a beauty contest which we suspected was a front for some illegal dealings. Even though the company turned out to be as fake as we suspected and we ended their criminal enterprise, my medal for best smile rested proudly in my safe. Not because it was valuable, just because it reminded me of a fun time in the midst of all the madness.

"Thank you, sir. I appreciate your understanding. Let me start with the first rumor as I'm sure it will be easiest to put to rest." I had their attention. "This is probably more of a timing coincidence, but some folks found it interesting that your brother," I gestured to Robert, "left town once Ted had graduated high school. It allows one with a creative mind to wonder if there was a reason besides being a great uncle that would make him stick around until Ted left for college." I hadn't come right out and said it with Dora Lee either. I wanted to be direct, but not any more specific than was needed. At least, as long as they picked up on my inferences.

Ted was the first to speak again. "The fact you heard my uncle was great at anything besides drinking and getting himself and the family into trouble shows your sources aren't to be relied upon."

I waved his concern off like I was batting an annoying mosquito. "So, he wasn't a good uncle? How about a good brother, then?" This time, my gaze landed on Robert. His face had flushed a bright red, but I couldn't be sure if it was anger, embarrassment, or something else.

"He was and is a troubled man who never understood the responsibility that comes with the Birmingham name. And, let me warn you before you make any further inferences; whatever you're thinking, don't. Consider your question asked and answered."

If it wasn't the truth, he and Dora Lee had certainly coordinated their stories and responses. Reaching out, I placed a gentle hand on his arm and nodded. "Of course, sir. My apologies. I should never have given credence to such a rumor." I hadn't really believed JJ was Ted's father, but I couldn't dismiss my suspicions that there was a secret this family was hiding that could help me.

Ted was leaning back now, his arms crossed. "Since you're so interested in the rumor mill and the untruths it's spitting out, one might be inclined to ask about the stories surrounding you in town over the past few days."

He had a point. What was the expression? What's good for the goose was good for the gander? Maybe there was another way to put the cliché in Texas, but his questions were valid. The least I could do was provide him a straight-forward answer. "You're right. I assume the rumor you're referring to is that I was responsible for killing Jonathan?"

Ted nodded, ignoring the look of warning his father sent his way. I'm sure he was more worried about me as an investor rather than me personally, but I was happy to dispel this rumor. I focused fully on Ted. "I know circumstances and timing certainly make it look like I'm the one most likely responsible for his death, but I swear on my family's honor that isn't true. I was with him the night he died, but I left him very much alive. He made a pass at me, I reacted, and like any woman who was being pressured would do, I pushed him away. When I left, he was walking away, laughing." I decided to leave out any more details involving Lester or EZ. "I hope you will believe me just as I'm trusting you."

Ted waited several long seconds before responding. I just hoped I'd won the internal battle going on in his head. "Fair enough. Any more questions?"

I had one more area I wanted to cover but needed to tread carefully. I wouldn't come right out and ask if Ted was

Jonathan's father, though that's what I really wanted to learn. "Almost done, I promise."

His nod was curt, but I took it as encouragement to continue. "Since you mentioned Jonathan, I've heard he had made it a goal of his to cause difficulty here in Wilson. From all accounts, you were the only one who truly tried to help him. Mrs. Birmingham told me earlier today that your family loved his mother, Lydia, and was very sad when she left without any explanation. Do you think her departure somehow fueled Jonathan's vendetta?" I'd tried to make my inferences without being direct. From all I had been able to glean, Lydia became pregnant, then a short time later she, Ted, and JJ all left town. One or more things could be tied together. Something deep inside made me believe this was an important part of the story.

The anger didn't flash in Ted like I thought it might, especially since he was already defensive. He leaned forward again, his gaze earnest. "You must believe us when we tell you that Lydia was a part of our family. We were all upset when she wanted to leave. I have no idea why, but she was determined."

"Based on the sizable severance package you gave her, I certainly believe your family held her in high regard." I directed this toward Robert as I didn't think Ted would have been given access to the family money at that point. At least, not enough to allow him to make a payout to her without anyone else knowing.

Robert's face appeared confused. "We gave her one month's pay to honor the years of service her family had given to ours. While we were generous, I certainly hope you don't consider that sizable." His reference humored me as I'm sure he was worried he was wasting his time answering questions from someone who was going to invest the equivalent of one month's maid salary with his bank.

Of course, a Birmingham's idea of sizable and a single household employee's idea would likely be very different. I'd known from my father she'd paid cash for the house and received a monthly payout from a shell corporation. I didn't want to play that hand just yet. "My sources indicated it was seventy-five-thousand-dollars."

Both men appeared taken aback by the number I tossed out. Robert was the first to recover. He shook his head and chuckled. "We were generous, but not *that* generous. Where did you hear such a preposterous story?"

"From a source much more reliable than the rumor mill, I assure you." I sighed. "However, I believe you when you tell me the money didn't come from the Birmingham family." And I really did believe that, but I hoped my father could confirm that once he heard back from his sources. Follow the money. It was always the best way to find out who was really behind any criminal activity or enterprise.

"You'll finish the investment paperwork, then?" Ted asked as he stood, indicating he was done with this meeting even if I wasn't.

Lucky for him, I'd asked all the questions needed in my quest to understand the bigger story behind Jonathan and his mother. I stood as well, but there was one more detail burning a hole in my brain that I wanted to close up. Focusing solely on Ted, I asked about it. "I'm still curious why you were helping Jonathan when no one else would. Was he blackmailing you for some reason? Given all the opposition he faced in the community, why would you jeopardize it all for a family that walked out of your life decades ago and whom you never heard from again until he showed up in your town?" I put up my hand to forestall the initial denial I knew would come. "Don't tell me he would never blackmail anyone because I know for a fact that was one of his favorite activities."

Ted sighed as he rubbed his face, then shrugged. "He wasn't blackmailing me. He simply asked for my help and shared his vision for Wilson. I liked the ideas he had and wanted to support him. Sometimes, change is hard but that doesn't mean it isn't necessary."

I nodded. "Change can be painful but often needs to happen. Thank you both for your time and for allowing me to ask my questions. I know you were well within your rights to have me escorted from the building." I hesitated for a moment. "I also thank you for at least considering my innocence in this whole Jonathan issue. I'll return to Kelsey now and have her finish the paperwork and arrange for the funds to be made available."

They both smiled. Robert extended his hand, and I shook it to seal the deal. "Thank you, ma'am. You've got gumption. I'll give you that."

He might not feel the same way once he got home and heard about Dora Lee's day, but by that time, hopefully they'd both be sipping their cocktails and laughing it off as another nosey person who had to learn more about the first family of Wilson.

I went back into Kelsey's office. She looked as nervous as a lamb in a den of wolves. Smiling, I reassured her. "All is well. At least as far as your job and new investment sale is going."

"No answers for you?"

Sighing, I took the seat I'd occupied before. "They answered me, but only left me with more questions. All roads point to the Birmingham family, but the logic and motive don't support it. Even if JJ was Ted's father, and Ted was Jonathan's."

"You think Ted was Jonathan's father?"

"The timing seems coincidental, but even if it's true and Jonathan knew–and I don't know how he could unless his mother told him–and he was blackmailing the family to keep the secret, then there's a motive for murder. But Ted seemed genuinely interested in helping Jonathan with his greater vision for Wilson. So, again, even if any of the parentage stuff is true, where's the motive for murder?

The entire situation perplexed and frustrated me. "Maybe I'm barking up the wrong suspect tree and need to refocus on EZ or the Bizzys."

Kelsey stood and came around the desk to place her hand on my shoulder. "Why don't you go on home? I'll finish up the paperwork and bring it over tonight with my favorite bottle of wine. We'll review any questions you have and then brainstorm motives for murder." She offered the last bit with a wry smile.

"You sure you want to be friends with someone who has to have those kinds of conversations over evening wine?" I asked the question with a rueful smile but desperately wanted to hear how she would answer.

She sat down in the chair next to mine and laser focused that intense gaze directly at me. "I want to be friends with someone who cares so much about other people, including herself, that she's willing to ask the tough questions or take risks to be of help."

Blinking away the gathering moisture in my own eyes, I wondered if Kelsey had any idea how true her words were? I'd put myself and my team in harm's way countless times over the years to help other people. It was part of my nature.

Even if Kelsey could never know the full truth, I liked that she understood that about me.

I reached across the distance and took her hand. "Thank you, my friend. I appreciate your kind words and the offer of wine and conversation this evening. Just text when you're on your way. I'll start having the money moved into an account where we can access it for the investment."

She squeezed my hand. "You know I'm not just saying all of this because of the money, right?"

I smiled and nodded. "I know, and that's just part of what makes you a wonderful human being and friend."

Despite the lack of answers and progress I'd made over the course of the day, I still felt pretty good as I drove back toward my home in Wilson. Not wanting to forget my promise to Kelsey, I pulled out my phone and opened the app that would allow for an encrypted phone call. Even though we'd developed a code to avoid problems if a phone call happened to be intercepted or overheard, it was always better to be safe than sorry.

After two rings, she answered. "Who would you like to speak to?"

"Peruzzi."

"Who may I say is calling?"

"Bardi." We'd chosen these names for when banking transfers needed to occur as those two families were prominent in the early banking days of Italy.

"The sparrow is secure?"

"Yes."

Though I'd established I was calling on a secure line, she continued to talk in code, which was fine by me. Even though this was for legitimate purposes, there was no point in changing what had worked for years. "How much feed does a sparrow need?"

"Eighty-five."

She waited as she knew I understood what the next question would be, but asking it would tip our hand. I pulled over to the side of the road and put my hazards on. Pulling up Google maps, I put in the bank's address and then did a long press on the location pin until the GPS coordinators came up. Next, I opened up my banking app and initiated multiple Zelle transfers to her: $30.38, $83.07, $95.70 and $30.72. She would know to use those to determine the location (30.388307,-95.703072) of the bank where the funds would need to be transferred. She would locate my account there and then deposit the money through a series of transfers that would at least help mask where it originated from.

A moment later, her voice came back on the line. "Feed will be delivered by the start of business tomorrow."

"Thanks, Peruzzi. You're the best."

"You know it." I could hear the smile in her voice, and it tugged at my heartstrings. I missed my team. We were still close and that would never change. We just couldn't be together right now, if ever again.

"Stay safe."

"You, too."

And with that, our conversation ended. Any warm thoughts of friendship and nostalgia slipped under the seat of my truck when I pulled into my driveway and noticed a man in a suit standing outside a Toyota Corolla. I decided to back into the garage. Not something I normally did at home, but it might come in handy if I needed to make a quick getaway.

After securing everything, I stepped out into the late afternoon sun. There was a small gleam of satisfaction at the sheen of sweat on the man's face. He obviously wasn't from here. The direction of the sun kept his face hidden in the shadows, so it was hard to see his features or expressions. "Can I help you?"

"No, and I'm not really here to help you, either."

One had to admire his candor. "Then why are you here?"

"I just had to meet the woman accused of killing my client and good friend."

Now, we were getting somewhere. "You're Jonathan's attorney." It was a statement rather than a question. "For the official record, I've been charged with nothing, which is good, since I didn't kill him. Now, you've met me. Anything else?"

"My business here is about done. I just wanted to put a face to the name."

I moved closer so I could better see his face and to confirm my worst fears. He might not have known my face, but I knew his. That face had been all over our last job board. It was Derek Devenhart. He had somehow been involved in the ponzi scheme my team and I worked to bring down in North Dakota. The job that had brought the heat and forced us to go our separate ways. Forced me to retire.

While I'd always been in disguise during that job, including a wig, glasses, and clothing to camouflage my true body type, my face was my face. We relied on the human imagination and convincing people the things they saw were real rather than latex masks and other modern marvels of science that would hide your true identity.

I stepped back and over to the side a bit, hoping to cast myself in the shadows until this man left. He stared a few minutes longer, as though he was working through some things in his head. Fear clenched my gut in a vice grip and wouldn't let go. I needed him to leave. "If there's nothing else, then…" I left the statement hanging to entice him to fill it with a goodbye.

He'd made it to his car and had the door opened when he stopped. He closed it and turned toward me once again. This time, the confusion on his face had been replaced with clarity and conviction. "It's all coming back to me now. Jonathan mentioned meeting a woman who was going to prove very useful. At first, I thought he meant in his bid to take over Wilson, but now I know he meant an income stream."

My nerves put on their disguise of indignation, and I pulled myself to my full height. "I have absolutely no idea what you're talking about."

The spoken words didn't dissuade him in the least. An evil smirk appeared on his smug face. "You know exactly what I'm talking about. Your name, hair, and accent might be different, but the condescension in those dark eyes of yours—that's unforgettable."

Another metamorphosis took place as the fear in my body transitioned to anger. Ninety-nine point nine times out of a hundred, my flight or fight reflex always had me fighting. It was both a blessing and a curse. Moving into his personal space, I explained. "It wasn't condescension you saw in my eyes when I interacted with your friends who manipulated and conned my clients out of the future they'd worked so hard for. It was anger." I didn't elaborate further that I had never forgiven myself for not being able to tie this legal scumbag to the weight that fit so perfectly around his friends' necks and landed them in prison. He was a slippery snake, indeed.

"You are a self-righteous snob who believes it's all right for you to bend the law to serve your purposes, but not anyone else."

Oh, this guy... He made me want to tase him just to watch him twitch. "I only did that when the legal system, which you're supposed to be representing, failed. I served others, not myself."

He gestured to my beautiful lake home. "I'd say you did all right for yourself." Before I could respond, he continued. "But your days are numbered. I'll stop by the police department on my way out and let them know the will reading is complete but that I have a bonus gift for them." He gestured around the beautiful area I'd found to call home. "The good people of Wilson might like to hear about how their newest citizen bends the law to fit her own needs and that my client, God rest his soul, was just trying to warn her when he realized who she was, and to keep him quiet, she killed him."

While it was preposterous to hear the words out loud as they were about as far from the truth as one could get, it would ring logical for Chief "By the Book" and give him another pretty bow to put on the package of my guilt. Moving to cut off his departure, I summoned a smile that hopefully conveyed my willingness to do business with this scumbag. "Before you visit Chief Parker, perhaps there's a deal that can be made here?"

The silhouette of smug satisfaction settled on his slimy face once again. Ah yes, money talked, and he was fluent in the language. He wasn't a hard read at all. "I'm listening.'

I forced my tone and actions to radiate reasonableness despite the churning in my stomach over what I was about to do. "Jonathan had proposed a monthly payment in exchange for his silence. I'm assuming you're open to the same type of arrangement?"

"What do you have in mind?"

"Five thousand." It was a low-ball number, but I knew his type. He wanted to win at everything, including this negotiation.

"Fifteen." He scoffed as though disgusted by the number I'd tossed out.

"Seven."

"You're not taking this seriously."

"I assure you, I am." Honestly, I wasn't. I didn't have any intention of paying blackmail to this man, but I would make a one-time payment to buy me time and to put the wheels in motion to finally catch this dirtbag.

"Ten, and that's my final offer." He put his last card on the table, crossed his arms, and waited.

"Fine. Write down the account you want the money sent to. I'll arrange for the funds to be sent over first thing tomorrow morning."

Greed had a way of making people do stupid things. My plan was to use the account number he gave me to see if we could tie him to illegal activity. While my father could help, I didn't want to ask him for any more favors as that would send his worry meter into the red zone. I'd have to call on my friend and former teammate again. If anyone could handle the job, it was her. We might not have been able to prove this attorney was a first-class scumbag while on the job in North Dakota, but that was one loose end I intended to tie up if it was the last thing I did. He was the biggest thread we'd had to leave out there. I wasn't going to make the same mistake twice.

He handed me the paper. "If the money isn't in my

account by noon tomorrow, I'm making the call to Chief Parker."

"I understand how this works. I assume you do as well?"

The confusion that flitted across his face led me to believe he wasn't following my train of thought. "Yeah, you pay me."

"In exchange for your silence. If any of Wilson's finest, sheriffs from any surrounding county, a constable, or even a game warden show up at my door, the money stops." Though, if Jeremy showed up at my door, I might be okay with that.

"I'm not an idiot." He leaned in a bit and lowered his voice. "After all, you and your friends had to leave town without your biggest prize." His chest puffed out as a wide grin prominently displayed far too many of his artificially whitened teeth. "Me."

With that final challenge, he was in his car and pulling away. The moment he was out of sight, I pulled up the same banking app I'd used on my way home to make the identifying deposits for the first transfer. This time, I made similar deposits showing the account number I needed her to trace.

I dialed her phone number again after ensuring the call would be encrypted. This time when she answered, I skipped all the pleasantries from before and started with, "The big bad wolf is threatening the sheep." Every bad guy was given a nickname when we started a job. She'd understand who I was talking about.

"Are we giving the wolf a taste?" Which meant, was I going to pay the blackmail money?

"Just one bite over the minimum. I sent details for the meal." This approved sending ten thousand and one dollars in the transfer. Anything over ten grand must be reported by the banks. Because she also understood this was blackmail money being paid, she'd make sure the funds came from an account that we believed the authorities were watching and suspected was related to alleged illegal activities my team had participated in over the years. The double flag would hopefully bring attention to this scumbag and start putting him in the heat of the spotlight.

I heard some clicking in the background. "Details received. I'll take care of it and let you know."

"This is code red for a number of reasons. You'll let the others know?"

There was a long pause as she processed this. "Understood."

The desire to just talk to her like a normal person and see how she was doing nearly overwhelmed me. I hated that my retirement also meant leaving my closest friends. It was for their safety, though. It had to be done. Still, I felt the pull between the two lives. The one I left, and the one I was starting. But right now, I needed to focus and make sure Derek Devenhart was dealt with. Breaking only slightly from protocol, I finished with, "Thank you. I truly appreciate you."

A much longer pause. "You're welcome. I miss you."

"Ditto. Stay safe."

"You, too."

I disconnected the call, knowing I'd done all I could to handle this problem for the time being. Once the money was sent, my former team would work their magic in the shadows. The knowledge they gained would serve to tarnish and discredit Mr. Slime Suit Devenhart's reputation and hopefully tie him up in legal battles or land him in jail for so long that anything he might say about any of us would be dismissed as a criminal's payback. It wasn't pretty, but it was effective.

Once inside my cool and calming house, my nerves would not be settled. The danger clock inside my brain was ticking time off in a maddening way. I paced the length of my house several times, but it wasn't enough. I didn't know if a walk would help but I figured it certainly couldn't hurt. I grabbed a small backpack that had the ability to be strapped to my front. In it, I put all the essentials for a quick escape, if needed.

After setting the alarm, I headed out. Each route I'd chosen had a name. This time, I would take the forest path. While there technically weren't any forests in Wilson, there were several wooded lots which lent themselves to a vibrant deer population among other animals one didn't normally see throughout the course of the day. I gazed up toward the sky to a particularly tall set of trees and saw the eagle nest resting proudly atop the branches. Since it was midday, there wasn't much chance of seeing the eagle as she was more of a morning person, but it didn't stop me from looking.

I continued down the road. Some sections had sidewalks, others did not. This particular area had walkers hovering close to the curb to stay out of the way of traffic. Though I normally didn't listen to anything in my ear buds, I'd selected some soft meditation music this time to slow the walls closing in all around me.

Taking slow, deep breaths in and out helped a little. However, my zen was interrupted as the sound of a motor getting louder and louder filled my ears. Given what had happened in the lake, the sound put me on high alert. It didn't sound like a car, but regardless, I needed to see what it was. Swiveling my head, I turned enough to see Karen Bizzy heading in my direction with her gas-powered golf cart. She was staring straight ahead. I was in her line of sight. She had to see me, right?

Though there was plenty of room for her to move closer to the center of the lane, she was making little effort to share the road. I jumped up on the curb, momentum carrying me into one of those wooded areas I'd admired earlier. The napping deer were not impressed.

I watched as Karen drove by, not even looking back to see if I was okay. Had she been trying to run me off the road? If so, I expected her to at least turn around and gloat a bit at the success of her efforts. Instead, she continued as though nothing had happened.

The audacity of some people.

Focusing my thoughts on a problem I could solve, I followed the trail of gas fumes. I kept checking behind me to see if anyone else on the road might have nefarious intentions. Maybe the Birminghams had lined up a parade of people who would see to it that I didn't feel safe to walk the streets anymore.

I sighed. *Paranoid much, Sadie?*

Pushing the negative thoughts aside, I put one foot in front of the other, moving forward with purpose, refusing to let fear guide me. The trail stopped in front of the Bizzy fortress. Thankfully, I didn't have to buzz the gate to request entrance this time. The door to their three-car garage was standing wide open. A Range Rover occupied one third of the space, while a paddleboard and kayak rested against one of the walls in front of their jet ski. The remaining space served as storage with a pseudo workshop set-up and several boxes. Also occupying the space was none other than the Karen to beat out all other Karens. She was oblivious to my presence, watching her pull items from a box and then throw them against the back wall.

I confess, I was itching for a fight. I needed an outlet for all the pent-up energy surging around inside of me. Karen was the perfect person to pick that fight with. "Hey!"

She started, then reached into another container before whirling around and facing me. My arms immediately went up in a gesture of surrender as my gaze moved from the fury in her eyes to the Glock now pointed directly at my chest.

Chapter Twelve

"Whoa! Easy there." My voice transitioned immediately from picking a fight to preventing one.

"What do you want?" she asked without lowering the gun one inch.

"You almost ran me over back there."

She faltered a bit. "I what?"

As much as I didn't want to believe her, she seemed genuinely confused by my accusation. "Back there on Sycamore Street. I had to jump into the woods to avoid becoming a hood ornament on your golf cart."

"I didn't even see you. If you're here looking for an apology, then I'm sorry."

She didn't really sound sorry, but now was not the time to debate such details. One never brought words only to a gunfight. To be honest, I think the expression was never to bring a knife to a gunfight, but I figured the warning was applicable when I was completely unarmed except for the taser and pepper spray in my backpack. Exhaling slowly, my new goal was to get her to put the gun down. "Honestly, I'm here because this has been an incredibly frustrating day and I wanted to pick a fight with you for running me off the road. I believe that you didn't see me. You were staring straight ahead, not really seeing anything. So, now, I just want to make sure you're okay." And to get her to put the gun down. I really wanted that more than anything

She sighed and returned the gun to its original location. Why she kept a gun in a box in her garage, well, that was a question for another day. Not one I was even going to try to get her to answer. She pushed the intercom button on the wall. "Richard, honey, will you bring me a martini?"

"Yup."

As much as I didn't want to admit it, the apparent simplicity in Richard's life and his one-word answers held a great deal of allure over the complications of mine.

"You want something?"

As a matter of fact, I did. "Yes, please."

She pushed the intercom button again. "Make that two, honey."

"Yup."

While I wasn't normally a martini drinker, at this point, I'd take it. She gestured to some lawn chairs, and we moved over to sit. I was just happy we were out of reach of the gun. Of course, that was based on the assumption she didn't have other firearms hidden nearby. We waited in silence until the drinks were delivered. This was her house and her show. I'd wait for her to tell me what was going on.

After she finished about half of her drink, her gaze found me. "I'm sorry I almost ran you off the road. Truly, I didn't see you. I was...am very upset."

"You want to talk about it?"

Her reply was a bitter laugh. "Why not? It's not like you can do anything to fix this, either, but maybe if I say it out loud enough to the universe, something will come of it."

I shrugged. "I'll be honest. I have enough problems of my own right now, but I'm a good listener." I let the words drift off to allow her the opportunity to say something I could listen to.

She finished off her martini and Richard appeared with another one. My gaze flitted around the garage. I didn't see any cameras, but it didn't mean they weren't there. I did see a kayak with a bent shaft paddle secured against one of the walls. It made me wonder if she'd been the person I'd seen out on the lake the other day.

"Thank you. I'll be in shortly, make you a snack."

He kissed her on the forehead without any other acknowledgement. Maybe they were a match made in heaven. Once Richard was gone again, I returned my attention to her. "So, what upset you today?"

"I have a friend who works at the CIA."

Thankfully, I knew she meant Community Improvement Association rather than *the* CIA. "What did you learn?"

"Jonathan's attorney was in town for the will reading."

Now that I thought about it, why did he come all the way from North Dakota to read a will? Normally, that was only done for the family or people who stood to inherit something. Maybe that meant he had family here after all. "Since I'm assuming your friend didn't inherit anything from him, what did the rumor mill dish up this time?"

She cut me a look but didn't reply to my reference to the alive and well rumor mill. "She shared with me that none other than Estelle Zimmerman inherited the largest portion of Jonathan's fortune, including both pieces of property here in Texas along with the land and monthly stipend he received from the mineral leases in North Dakota."

"Wow. I had no idea they were that close."

Karen laughed. "Oh, I'd say they were pretty close." She leaned forward and narrowed her gaze. "You know how she makes her living?"

The implication was there, even if Karen didn't outright say it. "I do."

"Well, there you go. Ms. Estelle Zimmerman has finally managed to sleep her way outside of the trailer park." The disgust in her voice matched the look on her face.

As much as I wanted to argue with her, at first blush, that was exactly how it appeared. EZ had made no secret that she had a thing for Jonathan. Maybe that was her angle all along. Befriend him, bewitch him, get him to change his will, and then kill him. It would give her the means and opportunity to move up the social ladder and not have to work anymore. I gestured to the McMansion Karen and Richard lived in. "You have more than enough money. Why should it make you mad that Estelle inherited his fortune? It's not like any of the rest of us were in the running.'

The disgust on her face morphed to disbelief. "You really don't get it, do you?"

That was beyond obvious. "Apparently not. Please enlighten me." She made it very hard to play nice with her. No one besides my sister could annoy me as quickly as Karen had managed.

"She inherited the RV park, which means it's not going away." With her confession, she sunk back into her chair and sipped more of her second martini.

"How do you know?"

"Know what?"

"That she won't shut the RV park down? Running a business takes more than money, at least if you want it to last. Managing such a controversial piece of property may be more than she wants to take on."

She waved off my statement. "There's more to that one than meets the eye."

"How about the eye of your cameras? I couldn't help but notice some of them are trained directly at the RV park."

I might have expected my statement to make her blush with embarrassment about spying on her neighbors, but instead, she leaned forward, a classic "cat who ate the mouse" look on her face. "I have a right to protect my property and keep an eye on what goes on in my neighborhood. For instance, don't think I didn't see you over there the other day."

This was not a good development. While I'd hoped to put Karen in a difficult spot, she'd expertly turned the tables and had me back in the center of the guilt circle. Wanting to play it off a bit until I knew more of what she saw, I shrugged. "Sometimes, my walks take me there. It's a beautiful little outcropping where the sunsets are amazing. You probably saw me chatting with Hank. Nice guy. Great grill master if the smells coming from his grill were any indication."

"I didn't see you talking to anyone unless you were having a conversation with the recently deceased. What were you doing up on Jonathan's porch for so long, anyway?"

The specifics of her questions made me wonder what the range of her cameras were. They must not have seen the breaking and entering of his RV, which was the first bit of good news I'd had in days. "Just trying to get a feel for the man. Since I'm accused of murdering him, I obviously am trying to learn what his motivations were and who else might have had cause to kill him."

She scoffed at my statement. "Power and money motivated him. Didn't take a rocket scientist to figure that out. The rest of it was just for his enjoyment."

"The rest of it?"

"The man liked to find and push every button a person had."

"Did he find your buttons?"

She stood and glared at me, making me regret the question and quickly remind myself she had a firearm at her disposal nearby. "That is none of your business."

She was right. It wasn't my business, but I still wanted to know. He obviously irritated her just by his presence, but was there more? What was it she told me before? There's always more to a story than we think. Which brought me to another question. "Did you see anyone else go up on the porch shortly after I did?"

Her eyes blinked rapidly as her eyebrows lifted. I had no idea what emotion she was trying to convey. She shook her head and offered a close-lipped smile. "You are losing it, girl. How can you not remember talking to EZ while you were up there? She returned home and joined you on the porch not even fifteen minutes later."

While I'd initially suspected it might be EZ who found me in Jonathan's RV, hearing the confirmation out loud disturbed me far more than I wanted to admit. Needing to get away from Karen before she found a reason to go psychotic on me and seek out her Glock again, I waved off what she said. "Oh, that's right. My head has just been spinning these last few days."

She laughed. "You really are losing it."

I ignored her jab and asked one more question before I would make my retreat and go find EZ. "Since you have cameras trained on his RV porch, did you see anyone else enter or leave his area the night he was killed?"

Karen reclined in her chair, fully at ease in the power-play we'd engaged in. "Wouldn't you like to know?"

"I would. And don't think I won't mention this detail to Chief Parker. You could have seen the killer and have him or her on videotape." I knew without a doubt they were uploading all the footage to the cloud or something as it might come in handy for them someday.

She frowned. "I know that would make your life easier, but the only person I saw go near his RV that night is the same person who went there most nights."

"Who?" If she didn't give me a straight answer soon, I'd make a play for the Glock and try to persuade her to answer me before Richard came to her rescue. Part of me wondered what one word he would use to keep me from threatening his wife. That would have to wait until another day. I had bigger fish to fry. "Well?"

She smiled before taking another sip of her martini. She loved making me wait. "Estelle Zimmerman."

Chapter Thirteen

I left Karen in her garage as I contemplated whether I should confront EZ or not. As my feet slowly took me toward her RV, my mind thought back over the details I didn't know what the murder weapon was since I wasn't the one to kill him and that detail hadn't been released in the press. Either they didn't know, or they were going to use it to put the final nail in the coffin of whoever did it. Assuming EZ had the means, after the reading of the will, she certainly had motive, and since she lived almost next to him and visited him regularly every night, the opportunity was there.

So, why didn't I really believe she did it?

Then, there was Richard and Karen Bizzy. Again, the means were questionable, but given their wealth and determination, whatever the murder weapon was, I'm sure they either had it or could secure it easily. Their motive was hatred of Jonathan and all he represented. Living next door to the RV park gave them a reasonable opportunity, but I can't imagine Jonathan going quietly. Surely, if they'd been the culprits, their presence would have alerted his neighbors. It wasn't that they couldn't have done it quickly and quietly—anything was possible, and sadly, people could be very resourceful when it came to ridding themselves of their enemies.

As far as I was concerned, they were neck and neck with EZ in the contest for the top of the guilt podium. Not far behind them was Lester Price. Maybe he'd somehow lured Jonathan back to the marina. His body was found there, after all. The hatred motive was an easy call, but something didn't feel right about that, either.

Which left me with a big, fat nothing.

A sigh of frustration escaped me. Typically, I was better at getting to the bottom of who the villain was. Of course, I was used to working as a team. Should I survive this test, maybe I could form a new team of law-abiding citizens who didn't mind helping a reformed Robin Hood of sorts from time to time.

I'd almost made it to EZ's RV when the proximity alert went off at my home. Again! I pulled up the active cameras and saw two police cars parked in my driveway. A moment later, my doorbell rang. I pressed the button to allow two-way communication. "Can I help you, Chief Parker? I'm not at home."

He held up a paper. "We have a search warrant."

This was not good. "I'll be home in ten minutes."

While his face registered annoyance at the delay, he nodded. "I'll give you ten minutes, not one minute more. Otherwise, we're moving to execute the warrant."

I cut the connection and began to race-walk home. I still didn't run, though it did feel like there was a gun to my head this time. I couldn't fathom what they were looking for but had to assume they'd identified the murder weapon. Or, at least narrowed the search for what it was. Depending on how specific the warrant was, they might be able to go through my entire home. That would not be good. While I'd taken extra care to secure all evidence of my past life, someone with Chief Parker's attention to detail might run across items that made him ask questions unrelated to his murder investigation. I did not want that.

I made it home in eight minutes flat. Not bad. My breathing was a little heavy and my heart rate was racing, but I attributed it more to the search warrant than the cardio. "May I see the warrant?"

The chief handed me the paper as Deputy Matthews looked on with that smirk of self-satisfaction he wore so often. If they were going to take me to jail for this bogus murder charge, maybe I'd add aggravated assault of a police officer to the charges. At least then, I would know I was guilty of something (and that he had it coming!). Once I finished reading, I breathed the smallest sigh of relief. The search warrant was for a specific item, which meant there was no need for them to search for it at all.

I keyed in the code to the garage and waited as the door opened. Once visible to everyone, I pointed to the back wall where my kayak was suspended on a pulley system and my shiny new paddle was secured to the wall. "No need for searching. It's right there."

A small part of me also felt relief as I knew without a doubt my paddle hadn't been used to kill Jonathan At five hundred dollars of expertly crafted carbon fiber, there was no way I would have grabbed it to use, even if I *had* killed him. Which I hadn't.

As Deputy Matthews donned the gloves to retrieve it, a sick, fleeting thought crossed my mind. The other day my proximity alert went off. Even though I hadn't found any evidence of foul play, the garage was the one place I didn't have cameras installed yet.

What if the real killer had switched out the paddles? Mine didn't have any identifying markers and the color was not unique. Given everything that had happened, it wasn't unreasonable to think someone would try to frame me. It was also plausible that any of the people on my suspect list could have seen me out kayaking. Maybe even the person who tried to run me over with the jet ski. They would have had an upfront and personal view of my paddle before they sent me topsy-turvy into the lake.

"We have what we need. Thank you for your cooperation, Ms. Sabatini."

I waved off his statement. It wasn't like I had any choice. "If you find anything on there that incriminates me, you should know there was a possible break-in to my garage the other day. I couldn't find evidence of anything missing, but perhaps something was replaced."

Deputy Matthews swaggered into the conversation. "Did you report this possible break-in? Any cameras?" He pointed to the one camera, besides the doorbell one, I'd had the opportunity to install.

I sighed, angry at myself that I hadn't seen to all those details before I tried to start my version of a normal life. "I hadn't gotten to the cameras in the garage yet. None of my other cameras caught anything. And before you say anything, as I mentioned, nothing was stolen or appeared out of place. What exactly would I have reported?"

He shrugged. "Anything would have been more believable than this story. You'd think with all the time you've had, you would have something better than the old *I was framed* bit."

As much as it irritated me, he wasn't wrong. Sometimes,

the truth sounded completely lame. That was why cover stories—at least, the good ones—were always much more interesting and, frankly, believable. I returned his shrug. "Guess I'll have to hold on to the belief that the truth will set me free since my innocence doesn't seem to be doing the job."

Deputy Matthews laughed as he walked to the vehicle to secure the alleged murder weapon. I'm sure it was off to Houston, where they would do a forensic analysis to look for blood and/or other incriminating details. If confirmed, my paddle would become the official murder weapon. I turned to Chief Parker. "You do know I'm not the only person in Wilson to own one of those, right? I've seen them out on the lake. Are you gathering all of them or just mine?"

"If you're as innocent as you claim, you have nothing to worry about. If this comes back clean, we'll move on."

"Promise?"

"You have my word."

That was enough for me. I might not have trusted Deputy Matthews, but Chief Parker had a maturity about him and a way that inspired trust. Which was saying something since I inherently didn't trust small-town police. This guy was slowly changing my mind. I did attempt one last volley regarding the possible break-in. "While I didn't report it and have no camera footage to help you identify who came by my place that day, there is a record of the proximity alert going off. For whatever that's worth."

He offered a rueful smile. "Without cameras to prove it was a person, it could have been a deer, a child, or anyone really. Let your attorney know, though. It might help them offer up reasonable doubt in your defense."

While his advice was sound, it also saddened me. He might not be showing it like a neon sign on a dark strip of road, but I feared that deep down, he believed I did it, too. "How long do I have before the test will be concluded?"

"One or two days tops."

It wasn't much, but it gave me time. "Okay, thank you."

"Oh, and Ms. Sabatini?"

"Yes?"

"Don't leave town."

Once the police were off my property and out of sight, I grabbed the bag I'd had with me on my walk and jumped in the golf cart. While not fast, it was capable of going into places that cars were not and much more efficient than my race-walk. The day's events had left me exhausted, but I had one more place to visit before I could sleep.

The sun had started to set over the lake, casting shadows over the landscape. If I hadn't been so upset, I might have taken some pictures to capture the play of the light over the darkness. But there was no time for such trivialities right now. I was done being one step behind.

Thankfully, EZ's 4-Runner was parked on the gravel driveway provided for each occupant. A small part of me wondered if she would continue to live here or if she would build a house on the lot across from Pete and Kelsey's place. Maybe she would move away completely—start a new life somewhere else where no one knew her. Money could make people do strange things. I pulled the pepper spray out of my bag and put it in my front pocket. The taser got tucked under my shirt in front. A quick visual check confirmed that I needed to pull my shirt out a little more to avoid the items being seen. I decided just to untuck it completely. It wasn't fashionable, but at this moment, I truly didn't care.

I walked with purpose up the steps to her RV and pounded on the door. "EZ? We need to talk!"

"Pipe down! You're interrupting everyone's peace and quiet."

The gravelly voice called to me from the dock where EZ stood with her lighted cigarette. I should've known. Maybe she worked where she did to fund her cigarette habit.

I'd been asking questions all day and getting nowhere. I wanted the night to be different. This had to be the longest Monday on record.

Violence was never a first option for me. Typically, it didn't even make the list. But my patience was waxing thinner than my timeline. I stormed over to the dock and, before I could stop myself, I pushed EZ, causing her to take several steps back. "Hey! What in tarnation is wrong with you?"

"Many things, but mostly you!"

There was a mixture of surprise and concern on her face, but she kept up the pretense. "You've lost your mind, woman!"

"The only thing I've lost is my patience. With you, with this investigation, with this whole town!"

She took a long draw on her cigarette, then smiled. "Then, maybe you should leave. You've been nothing but trouble since you arrived."

Something inside of me snapped. I moved forward, pushing her shoulders once again. We were dangerously close to the edge of the dock now. My finger wagged in her face. "The only place I might go is to the police station, where I will let Chief Parker know there's footage of you with Jonathan *after* the scuffle he and I had. Which would provide proof you were the last person to see him alive. And..." I let the word draw out for dramatic effect, "since you were the only person who benefitted from his death, I'd say that gives you a pretty hefty motive, don't you?"

A moment later, she lunged toward me, cigarette and all. I tried to step out of the way, but she was fast. The impact of her body against mine knocked me off balance and I felt myself falling. Before I could compensate, I felt the edge of the dock under my foot. In a hail Mary attempt to not take an unscheduled dip in the lake, I grabbed the only thing I could reach...one of EZ's pigtails. She wasn't ready for that, either, apparently. Instead of my efforts securing my footing, gravity did what gravity does and pulled us both toward the murky depths of the lake.

The warm water of Lake Amore welcomed us into its embrace. I released my hold on her hair to use both hands and arms to bring myself back to the surface. I expected her to surface a moment later, but she didn't. Oh, dear Lord, what had I done? Scouring the surface of the water, I didn't see any part of her. While the lake was beautiful, it was a typical man-made lake and didn't provide a clear view to the bottom, which was probably a good thing. No telling what secrets lie within the depths.

I couldn't have EZ's death on my conscience. I dove down, feeling blindly through the water for anything that resembled a human. My lungs burned from the lack of oxygen, fueling my need to surface again. I couldn't give up! Just about the moment my chest tightened and threatened to explode, my fingers encountered flesh. Not wasting another moment, I grabbed hold and began kicking furiously to bring us both to the surface.

The cool air of relief brushed across my lips, I gasped in an effort to draw oxygen into my body. The fire inside slowly started to die down once air was coming in regular doses. EZ, on the other hand, made no such noise. Dragging her to the shore, I started CPR and prayed I'd found her in time.

Two breaths, followed by chest compressions, repeat. I kept this up for what had to be an eternity until she spit water in my face and started coughing. I wasn't even mad. Instead, I started laughing in relief. Sitting back on my heels to help her up, I asked, "Are you all right?"

She shook her head but sat up on her own. I continued, "What happened? We were only in the water for a few moments before you disappeared in the depths."

EZ pulled her knees up to her chest and wrapped her arms tightly around them. She looked so frail. "I like looking at the water, but not being in it. I almost drowned as a kid, so I've avoided getting in the water my whole life."

"But why live on a lake, then?" I was pretty sure I would have chosen a land-locked state.

My question made her lips curve in a small smile as she shrugged her shoulders. "I like living on the edge.' A moment later, her smile faded. "I had no idea how I'd react if I ever was in the water again. Now, I know. I panic and freeze."

Sensing she had a slight sense of humor about at least part of this, I chuckled a bit. "And apparently sink like a lead balloon."

EZ took the comment good-naturedly and started laughing. "Apparently."

She stood, and I followed suit. "Come on, I have some towels you can use to dry off."

"Thanks." We walked up the bank to bring us back to the RV park. EZ's home was clean, simple, and surprisingly decorated in subtle hues of blue. She handed me a large beach towel before disappearing in the back, and a small part of me worried she might have a gun hidden somewhere. This was Texas, after all. Everyone, except me, had a gun, it seemed.

I did a quick check of the waistband of my pants and my pocket, not surprised to find them both empty. Lake Amore now had possession of my taser and pepper spray. I had more, but they were tucked safely away at home.

EZ appeared before I could worry too much. She had put on dry clothes and had a towel wrapped around her head. "Sorry, I'm pretty sure I don't have anything that would fit you."

Grinning, I teased. "You calling me fat?"

Her deep laugh did my heart good, all anger from before dissipated. "No, just big boned."

"Ouch!" I put my hands over my heart to feign covering the proverbial stab wound.

She pulled a beer from the fridge and offered it to me. Normally, I stayed with wine, but today had been a day. "Thank you."

Once she'd secured one for herself, she sat down at the table across from me. "First, thank you for saving me."

"You saved me. I saved you. Guess that makes us even."

Her gaze narrowed. "You wouldn't have died, just had issues getting your kayak out if I hadn't helped."

"Okay." I smiled gently. "So, that means you still owe me, right?"

"What do you want?"

I sighed. "Just the truth."

"Truth is rarely what people want, but ask away and I'll do my best to answer."

"Did you kill Jonathan?" Figured I'd start with the big one and see how she reacted.

After a long draw on her beer, she shook her head. I could see tears glistening in her blue-gray gaze. "I know everyone thinks I did it for the cash, but no one was more surprised than me when that lawyer said Jonathan had left all the money and property to me. He was my friend. One of the few men I encountered that didn't want anything from me except friendship."

"You wanted more?"

She didn't answer, just shrugged. "Is that all you want to know?"

"No. I want to know why you were in Jonathan's RV the other day and why you hit me on the head. How did you even know I was there?"

EZ had the good nature to blush. "Finding you there was an accident. I missed him and wanted to just hang out in his place for a while. Weird, I know, but ain't too many folks who think of me as normal, anyway."

I waved off her confession. "Not sure who decides what normal is, but wanting to feel close to someone we've lost makes perfect and normal sense to me."

She nodded, "I went to use my key, but realized the door was unlocked. I grabbed a loose board Jonathan was going to use to repair a cracked one on his deck and moved quietly inside."

"Then, you saw me and what? Decided I should be knocked out cold without so much as a hello?"

"I didn't know it was you. All I saw was someone in his bedroom. It's not like you and I hang out enough that I'd recognize you from behind."

She had a valid point. "That's fair."

"I had no idea who you were, what you wanted, or if you were armed, so I decided to act first and ask questions later. You would have done the same thing in my shoes."

Depending on the situation, I wasn't sure I would have. My past success had been largely dependent on getting people to talk. They couldn't really do that when they were taking an unscheduled nap. "What was on the piece of paper?"

Before she could answer, there was a pounding on her door. "Wait in the back."

Other than being a prime suspect for murder, I wasn't sure why EZ didn't want anyone to know I was in her home. As I still felt the guilt for her dip in the water, I decided to comply. Standing, I grabbed my beer and double-checked there was nothing that would indicate another person was in here with her. "Say guida if you need help," I whispered.

"Gweeda?"

Her questioning look brought a smile to me. "Italian for help."

"Got it. Now, go."

I slipped in the back where her sleeping quarters were. While I expected leopard or some other animal print to be the primary décor, the hues of blue continued. Soft shades accented by bold strikes offered a pleasing vibe to the whole space and gave me a little more of a glimpse into the woman I was getting to know. Focusing my attention near the door, I listened carefully.

"Well, look who decided to descend from the heights of her walled compound to pay us lowly folk a visit."

"I didn't come alone, so don't think you can try anything."

I recognized the voice. Karen Bizzy.

"Good evening, Estelle."

"This is quite a surprise. The Ice Queen visits as well."

EZ's reference did me no good. I'd certainly heard the voice before, but I couldn't place it just yet. Pressing my ear closer to the door, I closed my eyes and tried to clear my mind so I could identify all the players.

"What do you two want?"

"To make you an offer you can't refuse," Karen shared. I could almost envision the smirk on her face as she made the statement.

"I'm listening." EZ did not sound impressed.

"We want to make you a generous offer to purchase the land the RV park sits on."

"No."

"Estelle, be reasonable. You have all the money you could ever want now. Quit that terrible job you have, travel, do whatever it is you've always wanted to do."

The gravelly laugh I'd grown to like filled the space. "Emma Jane, you don't have the first clue about what I want."

I found it humorous that EZ referred to Emma Jane as the Ice Queen. Silencing my internal humor, I focused on the rest of the conversation.

"Everyone wants freedom. From their past, from their nightmares, even from themselves. The piece of paper in this envelope, plus what Jonathan left you, will be all you ever need to have whatever it is you dream about."

"That may be what you want, Emma Jane, but Karen here, she wants to be rid of all of us. As you pointed out, I have all the money I'll ever need, and making sure I remain a constant pain in Miss Bizzy Body's rather large asset here will help me sleep like a teenager every night."

"Why you..."

I heard scuffling, but I waited for the signal that she needed help. She'd proven to be pretty scrappy (well, except when she was in water), so I wouldn't irritate her by coming to her rescue if she didn't ask.

"Ladies!" I heard the now known voice of Emma Jane.

"Gouda!" EZ shouted.

The mention of cheese caught me off guard. Before I could give it too much thought, she yelled it again.

"Gouda!"

It was then I realized she meant guida. Not waiting another moment, I opened the door and grabbed a vase on the way out to use as a weapon since my normal go-to items were taking a long soak in the lake.

"Enough!" I raised the vase above my head to clearly demonstrate my intent.

EZ and Karen froze mid-scuffle and Emma Jane's gaze widened and moved from my face to the vase. "I'm pretty sure the owner of this home and property wants you to vacate the premises."

Karen and EZ released their hold on each other. My newest ally grinned and picked up her beer. "You heard her."

Based on the heat in Karen's gaze, if she'd been a fire-breathing dragon, we would all have been scorched earth. "You are unbelievable. Traitor!"

Emma Jane alternated her stare between me, the vase, and EZ.

"I don't want to use this." I lifted the vase higher. "But you both need to leave."

Karen put the envelope down on the table. "Think about it," she offered before stepping outside.

Emma Jane moved closer to EZ. I moved to defend her, but EZ's raised hand stopped me. "It's all right."

Emma Jane bent down to whisper something in EZ's ear. Oh, I couldn't wait to hear what this was. A moment later, the woman was gone. EZ reached out her hands. "Give me the vase."

She sounded upset, but I had no idea why. I lowered the vase and handed it to her. "Sure."

She disappeared into the bedroom, then returned to the table. "What took you so long?"

Joining her at the table, I smiled. "You threw me off my game when you said gouda instead of guida." After studying her, I had to know. "Did you really need help, or did you just want Karen and Emma Jane to know I was here?"

"You're pretty smart for a young thing." EZ grinned before sipping more of her beer.

"What was Emma Jane's deal?" I totally ignored her comment about my age. "She seemed more concerned with the vase than me using it on her."

Several seconds passed before EZ finally answered. "It was a gift."

"From?"

EZ closed her eyes. "Her father-in-law, Robert."

The pieces of the puzzle started to come together. I asked the question that would get me what I wanted to know without asking *the* question. "You've known him for a long time, haven't you?"

She smiled softly. "Almost since the beginning."

I returned her smile. "That explains how you know some of the things you know."

She shrugged. "Like I told you, people talk when they don't think anyone is listening."

"I'm going to come back to that, but first, I want to know what was on the piece of paper in the frame."

"A combination to a lock at a storage facility."

This was interesting news. Whatever Jonathan had in there must have been very important to him. "You went there?"

She nodded. "He'd taken me there once before. I waited in the car, but I think he wanted me to know the place was his, just in case anything ever happened to him. Before you ask a million questions, it was mostly furniture that I assumed he didn't have room for in his place. Maybe he was saving it for when he built a house, or maybe it was from his childhood."

"You said mostly."

"There was also a box, which contained blackmail material and his birth certificate."

"Who was his father?"

She shook her head. "The father's name was blank."

"Ugh! So not even Jonathan knew who his father was."

She grinned. "Sorry. You got a bump on the head for nothing."

I ignored her little jab. She must have been feeling much better after her trauma in the water. "I'm convinced it's Ted Birmingham."

EZ dismissed my proclamation. "Once his parents had shown him the way, Ted was head over heels in love with Emma Jane. He's never had eyes for anyone else."

"So, not a customer of yours?" Hey, she was serving up some jabs, I could do the same.

"Ha! Ted would never be seen anywhere near The Foxy Lady. His dad tried to bring him when he turned twenty-one. He wasn't having it."

"Wow, I didn't know men like that still existed." Though, I suspected Jeremy was one of the good guys who would turn down a chance to go to such a club.

A gravelly chuckle let me know EZ agreed with me. "They are few and far between," she shared. "But just because someone seeks an escape doesn't make them a bad person. Usually, they're just unhappy."

She'd probably heard story after story about the lives of the men who sought escape. We could probably debate that topic for hours, but I didn't have that kind of time. "Gut reaction...who do you think is Jonathan's father? Even though none of them make any sense when you put the whole puzzle together."

"Meaning?" She'd set aside her beer and leaned forward, elbows on the table, eyes piercing straight into the confusion swirling in my head.

"Ted would make the most sense. He was the right age. Lydia was at the house all the time. He was the only one helping Jonathan."

"But?"

I sighed. "But everyone I've talked to shares about Ted's unending devotion to Emma Jane, despite her not feeling the same way about him."

"Where'd you get that information from?"

If I said it out loud, it would make it sound even more ridiculous than it did in my head. But this was no time for pride. "Karen Bizzy."

EZ scoffed at the name. "You can't believe anything that comes out of that woman's mouth."

"Being jealous over someone and loving them are two different things." Not wanting to debate this with her any longer, since I didn't think Ted was the culprit, anyway, I moved on. "I'm pretty confident it's not Robert." Though I was certain, I was curious how EZ would react.

A shake of the head was her immediate answer "I know you won't believe this, but when it comes to that aspect of the relationship, Robert is as faithful as Ted."

It was my turn for a shake of my head. "You're right. I have a hard time believing that."

"Haven't you heard that old saying? I might have spent all my money, but I can still window shop."

"So, you're just friends?"

She nodded. "Friends that offer a few benefits." She winked. "But never that."

Interesting. As she'd never been less than truthful with me, even if it wasn't what I wanted to hear, I decided not to prompt her any further on her relationship with Robert. "Well, that only leaves one male member of the Birmingham family. That I'm aware of, anyway."

"JJ," she supplied.

"JJ. He was around and then left right about the same time Lydia got pregnant."

EZ brushed aside my line of thought with her non-beer-holding hand. "I'm pretty sure that was about the time that Dora Lee put her foot down about him."

"Meaning?"

"Dora Lee was done with all the trouble and tarnishing of the family name JJ managed to do without even trying. So, she made Robert choose: her or JJ."

"He chose Dora Lee, of course."

"Yeah, it wasn't much of a choice, really. Robert met with JJ and told him to leave town and never come back since he couldn't behave like a Southern gentleman or a proper Birmingham."

And that was strike three. I was out of Birmingham suspects. I finished the beer, though it had grown warm. It wasn't going to sit well on an already swirling stomach. I'd have to go to my B list of suspects. One last detail to wrap up my line of questioning. "All of the proper Birminghams I've spoken to confirm they were incredibly upset when Lydia left. Is that your recollection of the scene at the time?"

EZ stood and grabbed another beer out of the fridge. "You want another?" She chuckled. "I can afford to buy as much as I want now."

Smiling despite the situation, I shook my head. "I'm more of a wine gal myself. Maybe you should try it sometime."

The beer cap made its way to the trash along with our empty bottles. "Like I told Emma Jane, just because it's not something you like, doesn't mean others can't."

"You're right. I stand–well, sit–corrected."

EZ shifted in her seat. "I only have Robert's versions of events, but yes, they were all very upset. They didn't understand why she wanted to leave when they could help."

"No such sadness for JJ, though?"

"Robert was upset. He loves his brother. Sending him away was one of the hardest things he's ever had to do. At least, that's what he told me."

I believed Robert probably told EZ things he'd never tell anyone else. "Why does Dora Lee tolerate you?" I lifted one hand. "No disrespect intended, but I can't imagine her being happy about him having a..." I struggled to find the right word without further offending her.

"Side piece?" She laughed.

I laughed a little. "Yeah, I guess that works for a description."

EZ sobered a bit. "I keep telling you, Robert and I are friends. I listen to him like a woman should listen to her man." She offered a slight grin. "And I dance in a bikini for him, but it ain't like he can't see that kind of thing on tv if he wants."

I tried not to picture EZ in a bikini. "True. So...'

"So, Dora Lee doesn't like it, but she also knows Robert's never going to do anything to tarnish the family name. His visits to the club are less frequent these days, but our friendship remains." Those gray eyes pierced into me again, making me rethink so many preconceived notions. I was certain they still held true for most men who frequented places like The Foxy Lady, but maybe there was another group that sought it out for other reasons. Who knew? EZ was like an onion. There were lots of layers to her–more than most people would ever take the time to peel back and learn what an intriguing woman she was–full of contrast and mystery.

EZ continued as I processed her words. "You'd be surprised. After the first couple of times, some of them want to watch the show and then have a drink with you while they talk. It's weird, but it pays good."

Before I could comment any further or do a subject change to have EZ walk me through my next round of suspects, her phone buzzed.

She read the text. "I have to go."

"Friends with fringe benefits?" I grinned.

The beer was dumped, sink rinsed, and her keys grabbed within a few seconds. "No. JJ's been arrested."

Chapter Fourteen

"Arrested? For what?" I asked as I looked around for any belongings that might be mine.

She shrugged. "Don't know. Doesn't matter. I have to go."

"What are you going to do, show up at the jail on Robert's arm and help him save his brother?" It wasn't the nicest thing for me to say, but their relationship really confused me.

"Don't be an idiot."

"I'm not trying to be. I just want to understand what's happening."

She opened the door. "It's none of your business, but because you're worse than an old dog with a bone, I'll fill in the blanks for that pretty head of yours. Robert will meet me at our spot. He'll give me bail money. I'll get JJ out."

This obviously wasn't the first time this had happened if they had a routine down. I lifted my hands in surrender. "I'm sorry. You're right. None of my business."

EZ followed me out. I started to make my way to the

backpack I'd dropped on the dock when this whole thing started.

"Hey."

I turned toward EZ's voice. Maybe she wanted to thank me again for saving her life? "Yes?"

"Stay away from Emma Jane."

"Why?" It wouldn't change my going to see Emma Jane if I needed to, but I was curious.

"You like to stick your nose where it doesn't belong. Trust me when I tell you this ain't one you should be messin' with. She and Dora Lee are great white sharks. They both came from wealth and married into it. They're going to protect it."

With that warning, she slid into her vehicle and she was gone. I retrieved my backpack, thankful all the contents were still there, including my phones. I secured the one I used to communicate with Jeremy and dialed his number.

"Hey, Sadie. Kind of busy right now. What's up?"

"Where is JJ Birmingham being held?" Ugh, I really was like a dog with a bone.

"I'm good, thanks for asking," he countered, and I immediately regretted my direct approach. "What makes you think I would know?"

I didn't, but since he'd told me he got alerts on the scanner when someone had been arrested, it was logical to assume he might know where said person was being held. "If I remember correctly, the county jail is just across the parking lot. Maybe you could find out?" My question was lined with a hint of desperation. If Jeremy was even half the gentleman I thought he was, and since I wasn't asking him to do anything illegal or immoral, I was hopeful he'd help me out.

"Give me a minute." The tone of his voice led me to

believe that while he *could* find out this information, he wasn't happy about my asking. I'd have to find a way to compensate him for his trouble.

After several minutes, I heard his voice over the phone again. "I called a buddy over at the county lock-up. He's being held there. Why do you need to know?"

"I need to see him."

"Not going to happen."

"I *need* to see him, Jeremy. We can pretend I'm his lawyer. His family has pretty much disavowed him. It's not like the family attorney is going to show up to represent him." Yeah, this time I was definitely asking him to color outside the lines of the law.

"Are you an attorney?"

I grinded my teeth and exhaled a slow breath. "I am not, but since he's being held well outside the town of Wilson, no one but you and I will know."

A long sigh was his initial response to my statement. Whether it was from frustration, exasperation, or disappointment, I couldn't be sure. "I'm sorry, Sadie. I can't do that. It would mean I was perpetuating a fraud. I won't break the law or go against my own code, not even to help you."

His answer equally annoyed and impressed me. "Believe it or not, I can respect that and you even more than I did before. Which is a lot."

"Please don't ever ask me to do something like that again, okay?"

Though not sure I could keep the promise, I answered. "I'll do my best."

He chuckled. "Guess I'll take that. Is there anything else I can do to help?"

"How is JJ?"

"Even though my building is right across the parking lot from the jail, it's not like we have camera access or anything." There was a long pause. "My buddy did share with me he was brought in on a drunk and disorderly charge."

This was not surprising. His reputation seemed to be limited to drinking and carousing with women. "Fun times."

"All part of the job, I guess. Listen, I'm sorry. I really do have to go."

"I understand. Thanks for taking my call. You're still going to take them in the future, right?" My breath remained caught in my chest as I waited for his answer.

"I will."

The long, slow exhale felt really good, along with Jeremy's agreement to continue our friendship, such as it was. "Thank you."

"You're welcome." There was a small pause. "Hey, Sadie?"

"Yes?"

"I don't know if this will help you or not, but my buddy thought it was odd that all JJ's been doing after he asked us to call his brother is pacing the cell and repeating, *I didn't know, I didn't know.*"

This was an odd development. "Any idea what that means?"

"Not a clue."

"Do you know where and when he started drinking?" I figured that might at least give me a direction.

"No, but from what I recall in the past, he likes to hang out in local dive bars. Given his reputation, it's probably safe to say he'd been at it a while before he was brought in. That means it will probably take a bit for him to dry up enough for any rational conversation."

"Okay, thanks, Jeremy. Truly, I appreciate your help. Maybe we can have dinner again when all this blows over so I can show my gratitude."

He laughed. "Maybe one of these times, you'll actually let me do the asking."

Something in his statement warmed my heart. There still wasn't much of a future for us besides friendship, but I really liked that aspect of our relationship. I mean, it was the only aspect we had, but still, I liked it. "Maybe," I teased.

After hanging up with Jeremy, I closed my eyes and tried to mentally add these new details I'd learned to the ones already swimming around in my head. Hopefully, my dip in the lake didn't cause any of those details to get lost. This couldn't be a coincidence. JJ hadn't been in town, from what I could gather, for a very long time. I remembered Jeremy mentioning another drunk and disorderly arrest right around the time of Jonathan's death. It could mean something...or could mean nothing. As was the usual case, by the time I let new details get added into the mix, I always needed more to make sense of it.

The only person who could give me those answers was JJ, but I had no way to get in to see him. I twisted my head from side to side to pop my neck and relieve some of the tension. EZ and Robert were the only ones who would be allowed to see him. Of course, I had no way to reach either of them. Getting access to Robert was out of the question. But EZ...I might have a chance with her.

Making my way further into the RV court, I found the lot and grill where I'd first met Hank. I walked up to his front door and knocked. A few moments later, Hank's frame filled the door. "Well, hello again. Come by to take me up on the steak? We had an early dinner, but you're welcome to come back another time."

His warm smile was contagious and lit up his round face, making his green eyes sparkle like jade in the sunlight. "I'm going to take you up on that offer someday, I promise. For the moment, though, I was wondering if you could help me with something else?"

"Shoot."

"I really need to talk to EZ, but I realized she'd not given me her cell number before she left on an errand a short time ago. Any chance you have it?"

He nodded, his mop of brown hair moving easily with the motion. "Sure thing. We have a community cellphone list. Pretty sure she's on there. Gimme a sec."

As I waited, I thought about how close this group of people had become. A community who looked out for each other. Neither Karen Bizzy nor Emma Jane understood that. They had small, elite circles in which they had to meet some unspoken set of rules to be allowed in. These folks just happened to place their homes next to each other and had bonded over that. I vowed to myself then and there, I would do everything I could to ensure no one ever broke this group of people up by forcing them to move.

Hank appeared at the door with a piece of paper containing the number I needed. "Here you go. Hope you're able to get a hold of her. The missus says she usually takes a while to call back."

"Thank you, Hank. I really appreciate this. You've shown me a lot of kindness from the first time we met."

He shook his head and smiled. "It's nothing. We're all in this big world together. Gotta help each other out, right?"

"Absolutely. If there's anything I can ever do to help you or anyone here in your community, please don't hesitate to ask." I handed him one of my business cards from Tesoro that provided my legitimate contact information on it. "My number and email address are on the card."

Hank looked it over and tucked it in his pocket. "Thanks. And who knows, maybe I'll bring the missus by the shop sometime. She likes pretty things. She married me, after all."

We both laughed. "I'd say she got herself a real jewel. You've earned yourself a twenty percent discount anytime."

He nodded. "Thanks!"

I walked toward the park exit, then stopped at the end of the lane to call EZ. I realized she wouldn't recognize the number and most likely wouldn't answer. I sent a quick text first.

EZ, it's Sadie. Please pick up when I call. Important question.

I waited a couple of minutes to give her time to see the text, then I dialed the number. She picked up on the first ring. "Kinda busy here. What?"

"Can you find out when and why JJ started drinking?"

"Why does it matter? He–" She started to say something, but stopped. Her voice was hushed, so maybe Robert was close by?

"It might not matter, but it might explain something. Also, I hear he keeps repeating that he didn't know. Can you find out what he means?"

"You ask a lot," she whispered with irritation.

I hated to do it, but these were desperate times. "Pretty sure you owe me."

"Ugh. Fine. I'll see what I can find out."

"Thanks, EZ." Then, because I couldn't resist, I added, "Give Robert my best."

She disconnected the call without another word. We

were totally going to be good friends. I just knew it. That thought kept a smile on my face despite the situation as I slid in my golf cart and headed home.

Once there, I grabbed a yogurt from the fridge before deciding against it. I'd burned a lot of energy and deserved something with a few more calories. I grabbed a quick protein bar. It wasn't my choice for calories, either, but I needed something substantial to put in my stomach before I ingested copious amounts of sugar. Up next was the box of Texas gold bars I'd purchased from Tessa and allowed myself to indulge in. Mmm, that was good. This could become a dangerous habit for me, but depending on how things played out, it could be the last one I got for a while.

I made myself an espresso and curled up on the couch to make my next call. After a few rings, my father answered. "Hello, bella."

"Hello, Papá. How are you?"

"Smart enough to know the only reason you're calling now is to see if I have answers for you."

I blushed at his assessment, knowing he was right. We typically had scheduled times that we connected, and it was outside that time. Our pattern over the years had taught him that if I called any other time besides the prearranged ones, it was because I needed something. "I'm sorry. And you're right, as always."

He laughed. "Not always. Just ask your mother."

My heart felt better just talking to him. I believed that was one of the most important roles a father could do–ease their children's minds and hearts. "You're always right when it comes to me."

He chuckled. "I'll take that win." There was a pause. "However, I'll have to wait for the win on the information I know you want. I've connected with my source to try to trace the money and see what company was behind all the transfers through the various shell companies before it finally ended up in Lydia's bank account."

This was not the news I needed or wanted to hear, but it was progress, at least. I only hoped it would arrive in time. "ETA?"

"They hope by the end of business today."

Depending on where his source was, that could mean many different things. Asking would only serve to further frustrate me and annoy my father. He'd promised the information and would deliver it as soon as he had it. He knew it had to be important because he knew me. "Okay, thank you, Papá. I owe you one."

"You owe me many, my Sadie, but I hope there is never a need to collect."

"You're right. I love you."

"I love you, too. Be careful. Anyone who went to such lengths to hide this money will not appreciate you finding the source."

"I know, and I promise. As soon as you learn can you please text the information to me?"

"Ugh, Sadie. You know how I hate texting."

My smile wouldn't be contained. He did hate it, but I knew that I might not be able to take the call when it came in and I desperately needed this information. My Texas gold bar filled gut told me whoever paid that money had to be behind all of this. It was the only thing that made sense. "I know, but..."

He sighed and then mumbled something in Italian under his breath that I couldn't quite translate. It was probably for the best. "All right, my daughter, I will."

"Thank you. Give Mammá a hug for me."

"I will."

"You'll call again soon? You know your mother always enjoys speaking with you." There was a slight reprimand in his tone, and I couldn't blame him. Our last couple of calls had been more about me trying to get information than to just visit and catch up on each other's lives.

"I promise I will."

He sighed. "I just hope the call isn't from a jail cell."

His words sobered me. "Me too, Papá, me too. I promise you, though. I didn't do what they might say I did."

"Even if you did, bella, it would be for a good reason. However, I'm glad that is not the case. If you do end up in jail, I'm confident it will be a mistake. I know you. You'll find a way to make it right. You always do. Just, please, be careful."

My eyes glistened at his words. He did know me. While he may not know all the details of my life, he knew my actions over the past decade or so were to right the wrongs in the world. Wrongs that no one else seemed to care about. "I love you."

"I love you, too."

With those words, our call ended. I'd just given myself a few minutes to decide what I should do next when my doorbell rang. Pulling up the camera, I saw Emerson standing there. He was a great kid, but now wasn't a good time. I opened the door and smiled. "To what do I owe this wonderful surprise?"

"My aunt and I were worried about you when you didn't open the shop today."

I smiled at their kindness. "I appreciate that, but it really wasn't necessary."

Being a teenager, he didn't get the hint that I didn't want any company at this moment. I enjoyed visiting with him at the shop and appreciated the help and introductions he'd given me, but things were heating up and I wanted—even needed—to make sure he was safe. "Why weren't you at your shop today? Is everything okay?"

"I'm hanging in there. It's been a day." I continued to stand in the doorway as a subtle indicator that now wasn't a good time for a visit, but he didn't pick up on that. Whether it was intentional or not, I couldn't be sure. "Again, thank you for checking up on me. I'm sure you should probably be getting back to help your aunt."

He nodded, but he didn't move. "Can I have some sparkling water first? I'm parched."

Stifling a sigh, I moved to allow him entrance. "Of course. Let me get that for you and then I'm happy to drive you back to the flower shop so you don't have to walk in this heat."

Once in the kitchen, I handed him the water. He took a long swig. "Thanks, Sadie. What have you been up to today?"

His genuine curiosity made me pause and think about how I could describe my day. Nothing for a teenager to be bothered with, that was for sure. There was no way he would accept a non-answer, though, so I opted for the high-level version of the truth. "I'm desperately trying to prove my innocence. I'm getting close, but I need to find someone who has been around Wilson for at least as long as Robert and Dora Lee Birmingham have."

Emerson shrugged. "You can ask my auntie. She's been here for a long time. She and Ms. Dora Lee have been playing cards together for as long as I can remember. Maybe even before."

"Do you think she would see me today?"

"Why wouldn't she?" The innocence in his tone reminded me he'd not been jaded by the manipulations of people who have ulterior motives as their guiding principles. Though, in fairness, his aunt hadn't struck me as one of those types of people, either. I guessed I would find out how loyal she was to Dora Lee.

I smiled and shook my head. "No reason. Let me grab a few things, then we'll go see her."

I could feel his gaze on me as I put away things in the kitchen and then went to the hall closet to pull out a larger backpack. This one contained all the essentials I would need to disappear for a while if the need should arise. I'd bent the law many times, even broken a few in the name of justice for my clients, but going down for a murder I didn't commit wasn't in my repertoire. No one had ever died in my pursuit of justice. This was a whole new level. I wasn't running, simply being prepared to hide for a bit as I continued my search for who really killed Jonathan and, most importantly to me, why. He was no saint, but no one deserved to go out like that. Worst case scenario, he should have been arrested for his blackmailing attempts and paid his debt to society, whatever that was, for his crimes.

"Ready?" Emerson's voice cut into my musings.

"Ready. Go jump in the truck and we'll be on our way."

Once Emerson was in the garage, I did a final visual check to make sure everything was put away. A quick glance at my phone showed I had a missed call from a number I didn't recognize and a voicemail. Quickly, I retrieved the voicemail. The voice on the message sounded remarkably like Deputy Matthews, my least favorite law enforcement officer.

"*Tick tock. Time is running out.*" Though a brief message, I knew his intent was to rattle me. It worked.

I glanced back at my new home. While I wished I had time to wipe everything down, I couldn't explain that to

Emerson, so it would have to wait. Deputy Matthews had been wrong before, but maybe this time...

Hopefully, Emerson's aunt could give me some answers, or at least send me in a direction to help put this all behind me once and for all.

Chapter Fifteen

Emerson made the ride over to Wilson Floral with me in silence. He was a perceptive kid. Maybe he sensed things were coming to a head as well. Or maybe he was the strong, silent type. I backed the truck into a spot that would get me out on the road quickly. Always be prepared. The Boy Scouts and I had the same motto.

Isabella looked up from an arrangement she was working on when the door chimed. "Ms. Sabatini, what a surprise. I'm glad to see you're all right. Emerson and I were a little concerned when you didn't open the shop today."

"Sadie," I corrected and then added with a smile, "Thank you for checking up on me. Things have been a little crazy today. I brought Emerson back so he wouldn't have to walk, and I did promise to stop by, didn't I?"

She nodded. "Yes, you did. What can I help you with?"

Trying to exhibit a little more patience, I took a few minutes to walk around the shop and admire some of the displays. I was drawn to a bouquet of blues and white. "What are these? Are they the bluebonnets I've heard so much about?"

Isabella joined me and lovingly adjusted a couple of the flowers in the bouquet. "Sadly, no. Those are more spring flowers. The blue ones are wildflowers that I found, and the white ones are the Texas star hibiscus flowers. I thought they were beautiful and would go nicely together."

"You have a great eye. As a matter of fact, I think some of these arrangements would complement my jewelry. I'd like to order four or five like this to use in my shop. Can you do that?"

Her green eyes lit up along with the smile on her face. "Of course. Let me write up the paperwork. I can work on them and deliver them tomorrow." She glanced at Emerson. "I'm sure he would like to help as well."

He brightened at her words. "Yes, ma'am. I'd be happy to help."

"Then, it's settled." I followed her to the table, and we sat while she began to write my order up. I waited, then decided to ask my question. "How long have you known the Birminghams?"

Isabella looked up from the paperwork and swept some of the white strands that had managed to escape from the bun of dark hair piled on top of her head. "Forever, I guess. At least twenty-five years, maybe more. Time loses meaning the older we get." Her head tilted slightly as her gaze narrowed in my direction. She probably suspected there was a reason for my asking. I couldn't blame her. She had no idea where I was going with my line of questioning.

"As the black sheep of the family, I know he likes to carouse..." I winked at Emerson and enjoyed the blush spreading across his cheeks. "Besides that, what can you tell me about JJ?"

A small glint of relief passed across her features. I was sure she thought I was going to grill her about Dora Lee.

That could come into the conversation, but I'd save it for a little down the line. She shrugged. "That pretty well sums it up."

"Did the family ever try to get him to leave because of the bad reputation he was giving their name?"

Isabella laughed. "Oh, yes, many times. Dora Lee engineered and arranged so many jobs to try to get him away from this area. Good Lord only knows how many favors she called in back then."

"What kind of jobs?" I asked, more out of curiosity than anything else. Now that she was sharing, I wanted to learn as much as possible.

"Oh, you know the type. Positions within charitable organizations, a seat on the board or other positions with companies that owed the Birminghams or her family a favor. The list goes on. But each time, he kept showing up like a bad penny."

"Except the last time..." I prompted.

Isabella put down her pen and looked up at me, a hint of sadness now present. "Yes, except the last time."

"What made that time different? From what I've learned, when he left, he didn't return until this past week. That's a long time to not see your family, black sheep or not."

"All I know is what the rumor mill churned out."

"Which is?"

She looked over at Emerson. "Why don't you be a dear and run to the club to pick up the dinner I ordered for us a little bit ago?"

"But, Auntie..."

"Now, please." Her tone left little room for negotiation.

He sighed. "Yes, ma'am."

Once Emerson had left with one final look in my direction, Isabella leaned forward. "You must understand, these are just rumors. Nothing was ever proven."

I nodded. "Understood." I refrained from smiling, though it was somewhat humorous she was speaking in a hushed whisper despite the fact we were the only two in the store.

"Around the time Lydia would have gotten pregnant, JJ went on a bender and may have behaved inappropriately."

My gaze widened and I lowered my voice to match hers. "Meaning?"

"Well, there was never any confirmation, and of course the family denies it, but..." She let the words hang in the air.

"He was inappropriate toward Lydia? Took advantage of her?" I tried using the same word she did, even though we both knew what she meant.

She nodded. "Yes, Lydia. But I don't know if he truly took advantage of her or not. There was something about that girl that tamed the wild beast in him. He was gentle and affectionate toward her whenever she worked at an event the Birminghams hosted. I've seen love in the eyes of another, and he was in love with her."

"Forbidden love," I added.

"Yes. There's no way–no matter how much the family loved her–that they would allow one of their own to have a public relationship with the help. Can you imagine the scandal?"

The effort to refrain from rolling my eyes took a large amount of energy. While it might not be as frowned upon in this day and age, a few decades ago, I'm sure she would have been right in her assessment. "What happened?"

Isabella shrugged. "I can't be sure. It's not a subject Dora Lee would have told me over cards at the club."

"Fair enough." I knew she had an opinion on the matter. I just needed her to tell me. "But..."

"But my guess is JJ probably told Robert and Dora Lee he loved her, and they told him it was out of the question. He got drunk, found Lydia for some consolation, and..."

"And took advantage of her," I finished.

"She turned up pregnant and left town. Whether conception happened that night or another, it was less than six months later when Lydia left. The rumor mill claimed she had a one-night stand with a stranger at a bar. To my knowledge, she never provided a name, never asked anyone for money, and didn't try to blackmail the family. She just left."

This revelation worked its way through my brain as I tried to process what this meant and if it changed anything, knowing JJ might be Jonathan's father. Both Dora Lee and Robert had denied giving her any money but a one-month severance. Their claims had seemed believable. So, either I was getting rusty, or they were highly accomplished liars. Maybe it was both.

While Isabella returned to her paperwork, I moved down the line of Birminghams. From everything I'd learned, I didn't think Ted had the cojones to stand up to his parents and demand money for Lydia, even though they were close. From what I'd witnessed at the bank, he didn't stand up to them now, so I couldn't imagine him doing it when he was heading off to college.

Had JJ learned the truth that Jonathan was his and came back to town to...what? Kill him? That didn't make any sense, either. Ugh. Still more questions that needed answers. And frankly, I was tired of waiting. I turned to Isabella. "Let me sign whatever you need me to sign and then we can arrange for the delivery tomorrow. Sound good? I have some business I must attend to. My apologies."

"But I don't want you to sign it before I've finished. That wouldn't be right."

I offered her a sincere smile as I reached over and laid my hand on top of hers. "I trust you."

She nodded. "All right, then. Sign here. You can always adjust the order later if you want."

"I appreciate that, though I trust your judgment in these matters implicitly. I've seen your work."

As I started to make my exit, Emerson returned. "Where are you heading, Ms. Sadie?"

"Continuing my quest for answers. Maybe I'll see you tomorrow."

His face scrunched up into something resembling a pout. "Are you going to tell me what Auntie told you or where you're going now? I can come with you." He added the last bit with a gleam of hope in his dark eyes.

"Not this time, but maybe someday I'll share what I've learned. Okay?"

He sighed, shooting me a look that indicated it was anything but okay. "I guess."

"Listen, I promised your auntie that I would respect her desire for privacy in this matter. You don't want me to break my promise to her, do you?"

"No." His pout continued for a moment longer, but then he smiled. "Someone will tell me if I ask enough people."

Despite everything, I laughed. "I know...because of that face. You're probably right, but I want you to remember something very important."

"What's that?"

"Sometimes knowing everything isn't always good.

There's a reason the expression *ignorance is bliss* is right sometimes." I leaned in, whispering, "Can you text me the address for Robert and Dora Lee?"

He nodded. "Consider it done. It's going to cost you either some information or another lunch."

I laughed, appreciating his negotiation technique. "Deal. We'll talk more later. Thanks, Emerson. Enjoy your dinner."

"Bye, Ms. Sadie. Please be careful."

I stopped long enough to turn back to him with a smile and wink. "I'm always careful."

While I would have loved to head straight to Robert and Dora Lee's address, I decided I needed to be more thorough with my home. Though it pained me to admit it, the voice-mail had me spooked and made me believe time truly was running out. As a result, it was important to ensure I'd done everything possible to buy myself more time, if needed.

Once inside my place, I slowly walked through the house and secured any item that might lead a curious investigator to my past life. There wasn't much, but it needed to be hidden away.

I collected any personal items that would easily lead to family, like photos and cards from a past birthday and put them in the floor safe I'd installed. While there, I secured a couple more burner phones. I also took a moment to put Jeremy's number in my regular phone. I may have to dump the one with the number he'd been using. Though I shouldn't keep his number or that connection, I just couldn't let go. I prayed it wouldn't be my undoing later.

Once everything was finished, the home resembled one that had been staged for sale. At least it would be nice and clean when I returned. I consoled myself that this was probably overkill, but one could never be too careful.

Before I left, I gifted myself a visit to my dock. The sun had started its descent over Lake Amore. Despite everything that had happened in the short time I'd been here, I enjoyed living in this town. I was even starting to make friends. Kelsey had shown me such kindness. I looked forward to our developing friendship. Emerson, Isabella, and Tessa had also been kind to me. Heck, even EZ and I might someday be close. I inhaled and exhaled slowly. No reason to be all doom and gloom. I was just being cautious.

I checked my phone one more time to see if anything had come in from my father. Nothing. Oh well, I'd delayed long enough. Time to get to the bottom of this mystery so I could get on with my life.

Once in my truck, I made my way to the address Emerson had provided. While I was in the lakefront part of the community, there was also a golf course area. Here, the McMansions sprawled over more than one lot, which lent itself to affluence. Property wasn't cheap, so owning multiple lots indicated there was money to spare. The Birmingham estate sat on at least two lots next to a well-maintained and pristine hole on the golf course. I had no idea which one, as golf had never been my sport, but the landscaping blended beautifully and gave the appearance that their yard went on and on. Besides manicured lawn and bushes, many of the same types of flowers I'd seen in Isabella's shop were displayed here in their natural environment. There was also a four-car garage. Yes, this was definitely worthy of the Birmingham name.

I rang the doorbell, fully expecting a maid or butler to answer the door. To my surprise, Dora Lee answered. She was dressed casually in a pantsuit and blouse. I suspected this was as casual as she ever dressed, even in the privacy of her own home. Somewhere deep inside, I felt a moment of sympathy for her. Always having to maintain appearances had to be exhausting. Sometimes, I liked to just hang out in yoga pants and a T-shirt. I couldn't imagine Dora Lee in such attire.

She offered me a close-lipped smile, and I heard her exhale. I'm sure she was surprised that it was me at her door. Being the true high-class lady she was, she quickly recovered. "Ms. Sabatini, to what do I owe this unexpected visit?"

"May I come in for a moment? I promise not to take too much of your time."

She hesitated for a moment before her manners kicked in and she stepped back to open the door wider. "Of course, please come in. May I offer you a drink?"

While I would have loved a drink about now, I decided I wouldn't be here long enough to enjoy it. She would either answer my question and I would leave, or she would kick me out after I asked. "No, thank you."

We stood at the entrance to her grand living room. Every piece of furniture and decorative item was in the perfect place. It made my recently staged home look like a child had been playing Barbie dream house or something. After a quick survey, my gaze landed on Dora Lee. Her body language screamed impatience, so I decided to get right to the point. "Pardon my bluntness, but–"

She scoffed and interrupted me. "I've not known you to be anything but blunt, so ask your question and leave me to my evening routine."

I exhaled slowly to keep calm. I didn't want to fight with her. "I truly am sorry. Usually, I'm more discreet."

"So my husband tells me."

At the mention of him, Robert appeared from another room. Guess he and EZ had finished bailing JJ out of jail, or at least he'd delivered the money and returned home. A small part of me was amused that they actually had talked about me over drinks. Oh well, might as well move forward, then. "I've come to the conclusion that the only scenario that makes sense is that your family paid Lydia to leave to avoid the scandal of your housekeeper being impregnated by a Birmingham."

Her porcelain face flushed red, and I noticed her hands ball up into a fist. It was easy to guess anger flowed through her system at an alarming pace. Robert appeared calmer, but maybe he was used to people poking at him more than Dora Lee was. Men usually tended to be more direct than women. He opened his mouth to say something when Dora Lee cut him off with a glare. She moved closer to me, and I fought the natural reaction to step back to leave enough personal space between us. "As I told you before, we did no such thing. Her situation was a result of a one-night stand with someone she met at a country dance bar. We asked Lydia to stay, and we offered to help her out however we could."

The logical part of my brain searched for reasoning. "Then, why would she leave?"

Dora Lee exhaled slowly, but the redness in her face remained. "As you've been told, we have no idea. We wanted to help, even though she'd gotten herself into trouble."

A couple light bulbs started to dimly glow inside my head. "And at no time, despite things you'd learned from other members of your family, did you think her story might have been made up to protect your family name?"

"That is preposterous."

"People fall in love with people outside their class all the time. There's nothing preposterous about that."

Her arms crossed. "We wanted to help her. It's as simple as that. After all, what was she going to do otherwise? The story, as she told it, was believable enough. No reason for us, or anyone for that matter, to doubt it."

I watched her closely. She was telling the truth. Or, at least, the truth as she'd known it. She truly didn't believe JJ was the father of Lydia's baby...of Jonathan. Confused, I looked to Robert. His face held the same conviction.

But they had sent JJ away. Had Lydia been the final straw Isabella had shared with me?

Once again, no answers sent the beating drums in my head to a new level. I needed to get out of here. I needed to think.

"If there's nothing else, I'll thank you to take your leave." Dora Lee's statement left no doubt it was an open invitation for me to get the heck out of their home.

"Something isn't right here, and I'm going to get to the bottom of it."

"Dig all you want. We're telling the truth. You should stop listening to rumors and speculation."

I wasn't sure Isabella's version of the story counted as rumor or speculation, but she was only following the logic, too. "The truth will set me free." I quoted my now-favorite Emerson line. Though I knew he wasn't the original person to express the sentiment, it felt more personal coming from him rather than Jesus at the moment. Though having Jesus behind the statement gave it significantly more weight.

She walked to the door and opened it, leaving no doubt that it was time for me to go. "Have a nice evening, and don't come back."

Guess I wasn't going to get invited over for poker night, after all. I left without saying another word.

I moved my truck to a parking spot for a nearby dog

park, then got out and walked. I needed to think and clear my head. Had I been headed down the wrong path all along? If JJ wasn't the father...heck, if a Birmingham wasn't the father, then who? Not too many people possessed the kind of money they did to pay Lydia for essentially her whole life.

I'd only made it a couple of blocks when I got a text from Kelsey. *Where are you? I'm at your place for wine, remember?*

Ugh, I hadn't remembered. I owed her an explanation in person, though. I replied to her text. *Be there in a few.*

I walked back to my truck and made the quick trip to my house. I parked along the street as I still anticipated the possible need for a quick getaway. Kelsey was sitting on the steps leading up to the door, holding a bottle of wine. "There you are." She held up the bottle. "I'm ready to celebrate. Had a big investor earlier today."

I couldn't help but smile. "And that investor expects you to keep careful watch over her money and make it grow significantly."

She laughed. "It's what I do. Pete's not the only one who brings home the bacon. Owning two lots in Wilson doesn't come cheap, you know."

Honestly, I was ashamed that I'd assumed Pete was the main breadwinner. Very old fashioned of me. "You go, girl!" Instead of opening the door, I gestured to the path leading to the back of the house. "Let's sit on the dock, have a celebratory glass of wine, and then I'm going to have to call it a night. It's been such a long day."

She pouted but must've seen the strain on my features. "Okay, one glass and then I'll demand a raincheck."

"Deal."

We sat in silence as the sun continued its journey lower.

After a few sips of wine, I turned to her. "Thank you for being such a good friend to me. It means a lot."

She studied me before she responded. "You're a good person, Sadie Sabatini. No matter what the rumors may say."

I chuckled, returning my gaze to the water. "Oh, the rumor mill is going to be churning hard by morning. I visited Dora Lee and Robert just a bit ago."

She sighed. "You can't let it go, can you?"

"No, my friend. I cannot."

We finished the wine, and she gave me a hug before leaving. "Call if you want to talk about it."

"I will. Thanks."

She left me sitting there as the sun met the water and prepared to say goodbye to the day. I pulled out the burner phone and took a picture of the sunset. I texted Jeremy. *Wish you were here.*

A few minutes later, a text with a picture came back. I could see he was out on his boat and his view was even better than mine. *On patrol, but maybe soon. Talk later.*

I put the phone away with a smile. Jeremy Raber was one of the good guys. The sound of footsteps approaching behind me stopped my journey into fantasyland. "You decide you want one more glass?" I teased Kelsey.

When there was no response, I turned and found an angry looking Emma Jane Birmingham. She was dressed for kayaking and had her paddle—her carbon fiber, bent shaft paddle—held soundly in her grip. "Emma Jane, what are you doing here?"

"I came to give you one final warning. Stay away from my family. Let this witch hunt of yours drop."

While I knew I should be afraid at the level of hate I could see in her eyes in the fading light, this wasn't my first run-in with danger. I'd faced fiercer foes than this socialite. "I'm sorry. I can't do that."

She started to respond when my phone buzzed. "Excuse me for just a moment."

It was a text from my father. As I read the words, my fear factor rose by a level of at least ten. I sent a quick text of thanks to him. Before I put the phone away though, I dialed 9-1-1. I didn't hit send, but I wanted to be prepared.

When I looked up at Emma Jane, all the pieces clicked into place. "It was you."

"What?"

I held up the phone. "It's not a rumor. Well, not an accurate one. Everyone, including myself, thought it was the Birminghams who paid Lydia to leave, but it wasn't. It was you—more accurately, the McIntyre family trust—who paid Lydia to leave. You left the Birminghams completely in the dark." I momentarily comforted myself that my human lie detector was still operational and accurate. Well, mostly. I'd missed any and all signs with Emma Jane.

"That's enough." Her grip on the paddle tightened. Her knuckles were losing their color from the effort.

"You were at Robert and Dora Lee's earlier weren't you?"

"We were having an evening drink and discussing how to handle our latest problem. You." She took a small step forward.

I thought back to my conversation with the senior Birminghams, what had been said and, most importantly, what had not. Then, the three words that JJ had been muttering over and over in his drunken state made perfect sense. Jonathan must have told him that *he* was the father. That's what he hadn't known. The last part was a theory, but I was willing to work with it in the heat of the moment.

"Everyone thinks Ted is the father. That's the only thing that explains everything and makes sense."

Emma Jane adjusted her grip on the paddle while I shot a quick glance around to see if any of my neighbors were out on their decks enjoying the sunset as well. Not a single soul. It figured.

"It makes sense because it's true. There's no other reason I would have gone to such lengths to protect Ted...to protect my new family. Our future!"

I shook my head. "No, Ted wasn't the father." I hoped EZ would confirm my theory soon, but until then, I was carrying out what might be the most important bluff–which might not be an actual bluff at all–in my entire life.

Another small step. She was now less than four feet away. "Once again, your sources are wrong. Ted got drunk. He had a one-night stand with the maid. I wrote it off as boys being boys, but then she turned up pregnant."

The shrug of my shoulders was minimal. I surmised there was only a thin thread holding Emma Jane to the reality she'd weaved in her head. Cutting it loose might unleash all manner of holy Hades against me. "I don't know about him getting drunk, though I doubt he slept with her. By all accounts, he only had eyes for you. Besides, he wasn't the Birmingham she was in a secret relationship with."

"You are a liar!" Her voice had dropped several menacing measures.

My head shook of its own accord. "No, it was JJ. He was falling in love with her, and his family told him it was out of the question. But when Lydia got pregnant..."

"You're wrong. Lydia told everyone it was a one-night fling with a cowboy she met at a dance bar, but I knew the truth."

All the information I'd gathered over the past several

days became relevant now. "No. Ted wouldn't even go to a strip club for his twenty-first birthday. He wasn't going to have a one-night stand with the help, especially when they were friends." I now believed their relationship had been purely platonic. It explained Ted's desire to help Jonathan so much.

"You have no proof." Another step.

I held up the phone with the screen facing me. "I followed the money. Well, I had someone else do it. Kudos to your family's accountant as it took even someone who is very good several days to trace the money through all the shell companies. Your guy was good. Mine just happens to be better. And now, I'm calling the police because I think Jonathan threatened to blackmail you with this information, didn't he?"

Rage flashed in her gaze, and I wondered if it was the same look she had on her face when Jonathan confronted her and threatened to make her pay to keep her dirty little secret. She started moving toward me. I hit send on the phone, hoping the 911 operator would be able to hear the scuffle and send help. I sent up a prayer that they would put all the pieces together in time. "That ungrateful excuse for a man. We'd been taking care of him his entire life, and he still wanted more."

"Maybe Jonathan tried blackmailing Ted as well. Who knows. That was his style. Either way, you found out about it, scheduled a meeting, and killed him with that." I pointed to the paddle in her hand.

"*911, what is your emergency?*"

Emma Jane heard the voice through the phone and with a primal scream, she lunged at me, the paddle swinging directly for my head. On instinct, I lifted my arm to deflect the blow. Pain ripped through my forearm and caused me to lose my grip on the phone. Now that both hands were free, I leaned into the fight and tried to get a grip on the paddle to get it away from Emma Jane. Her grip was strong for being petite and she was pure muscle. She jerked the paddle back and initiated another swing. This time, it connected with the side of my head, knocking me to the ground.

My fight or flight instinct kicked in. As she stepped closer to deliver another blow, I grabbed her ankles and pulled hard. She must not have been expecting it, as she came toppling down with a grunt. I rolled to try to gain an advantage, but she was quick. Evading my grasp, she grabbed a fistful of hair and pulled me toward her, the resounding crack against my cheek sending stars into my vision long before they were supposed to fill the night sky.

I'd had enough.

I grabbed her arms and pulled. We started rolling, toppling over one another until I felt nothing but air under my frame. Ugh, not again!

The warm waters of Lake Amore welcomed me once more. This time, though, instead of diving down to look for EZ, I felt a tug on my ankle as my body was jerked under the water. Before I submerged completely, I sucked in a lung full of air. I kicked hard, hoping to hit something solid and loosen her grip.

I missed.

My body twisted and turned until her hold on me loosened. This time, my kicks were designed to get me to the surface. Precious air entered my body, and I heard Emma Jane doing the same. Twirling in the water, I kicked again and lunged toward her. It was my turn to be the aggressor.

We clawed, slapped, and tried to gain a position that would allow one to send the other to the murky depths. Everything else in the world—the sights, the sounds, the normal serenity of the lake—faded away as I fought for my life.

Finally, I'd managed to get in a position of power and started to push her under. Her head had just disappeared when I felt a strong grip on the back of my shirt as I was pulled away from her. "No!" I screamed, desperate to win the fight. I clawed at the hand that held me hostage as the rest of me surged toward Emma Jane again.

"Sadie! Calm down. I'm here to help."

Somewhere in my blind rage of self-defense, a recognizable voice filtered through. The same one that had filled my dreams for days now. Once I stopped fighting him, he lifted me effortlessly from the water and sat me in the boat. He didn't say a word, but guided the boat closer to Emma Jane and rescued her as well.

I cast a glance at Emma Jane. She was strangely subdued and appeared smaller than the raging beast she'd been only moments ago. Jeremy didn't say anything to either of us. He handed us a towel, then moved the boat so he could tie it off at my dock. After speaking into his radio, he finally sat down in the captain's seat and gazed at both of us. I'm sure we made quite a sight.

"You two have a lot of explaining to do."

Chapter Sixteen

"I want my lawyer," Emma Jane began.

"You can call him or her once the authorities arrive and take you to the police station," Jeremy explained patiently.

I said nothing, but kept my gaze on the lake, avoiding eye contact with Jeremy. I happened to see Emma Jane's paddle floating nearby. I pointed to it. "You might want to retrieve that. I'm pretty sure it's the murder weapon."

"Who got killed with it?" Jeremy asked as he grabbed a long pole with a claw-like attachment on the end.

"Jonathan Kirkpatrick."

He cast a quick glance at me, then Emma Jane. In this moment, her physical frame was hunched over as she held herself tightly. The defiance in her eyes was still present, even as her world was crashing down around her. "You have anything to say about that, Mrs. Birmingham?"

Her angry glare shot laser beams of hatred in Jeremy's direction. To his credit, he didn't even flinch. "Lawyer," she repeated as though that would make him change his mind.

He didn't respond as I'm sure he believed that had

already been asked and answered. He turned to me. "You have anything to add?"

Unlike Emma Jane, I was ready to share what I'd learned, or at least what I suspected. "Some is theory, and some can be proven."

"I'm listening."

"Jonathan loved to blackmail people. It was his favorite activity, from what I've learned. I believe EZ has proof she obtained from a storage facility just outside of town of all the people he was extorting." I left out the part where he threatened to blackmail me. No sense in muddying the waters of the already complicated relationship Jeremy and I shared. That was for another day. I also hoped he hadn't had the time to add his notes about me to his blackmail box.

Emma Jane shot me an angry glare, but she didn't say anything, so I continued. "Everyone in the Birmingham family believed Lydia's story about a drunken one-night stand. They were wrong. It was JJ Birmingham. He and Lydia were in love, but the family had shut that down faster than you could say reputation. Lydia knew there was no way the Birminghams would allow JJ to be a father in any way to their child. JJ had to have been devastated when he thought Lydia had slept with another man. So, this time when Dora Lee forced him to leave, he stayed away. Everyone believed the story, except Emma Jane here. She knew Ted and Lydia were very close, best friends even, so she believed the drunken part of the one-night stand. However, she didn't believe the part about him being a stranger."

"You shut up!" She seethed.

I knew Jeremy wouldn't let anything happen to me, so I didn't shut up. "Emma Jane believed it was Ted, but he only had eyes for her. Which, honestly, I don't see the attraction but—"

"Sadie..." Jeremy warned.

"Moving on," I smiled up at him. "Emma Jane arranged for her family to pay Lydia to keep her silence. My guess was Lydia was scared. She was going to be raising a baby on her own and was moving far away from everything and everyone she knew. JJ had left. There was no reason for her to stay. Since JJ had believed her story, that's probably why he never went and looked for her."

"And you know all of this to be true?" His question hurt a little, but since he knew I could weave a story from time to time, I guess it was a fair question.

I nodded. "That's my theory, but I'm sure the police can confirm with him once he sobers up."

"Jonathan must have shared with him when he was back in town that he was his father."

I smiled. Jeremy and I made a good team. We thought alike. Well, maybe not exactly alike, but enough to work out details of a crime together. We had just been on opposite ends of the law to get the experience necessary to do so. Details, details. "When he learned, he realized all the opportunities he'd missed with Jonathan and Lydia. Heck, maybe Jonathan tried blackmailing him, too. But JJ wouldn't have cared if the truth came out. He probably would welcome it. Instead, he went on a bender that's landed him in jail twice over the past week for drunk and disorderly charges."

"JJ is an idiot." Emma Jane finally spoke.

I sensed my time with Emma Jane was ending, so I decided to wrap up my theory and see if she would confirm anything now that she was in a more talkative mood. I was certain she thought I was an idiot as well. "So, Jonathan knows JJ is the black sheep of the family and they'd never believe him about Lydia, so while JJ was drinking his sorrows away, Jonathan contacted Emma Jane here to try and squeeze her for more money."

Jeremy's face screwed up. "But he had more money than he'd ever need." He looked at Emma Jane, "Why would he risk everything to blackmail you?"

When she didn't respond, I offered up a theory. "Greed or revenge. Maybe he realized the life he could have had, even as an illegitimate son of a Birmingham. The oil money just happened in the last few months. While their needs were cared for by the monthly infusion of cash from the McIntyre trust, I'm guessing Jonathan realized how much he'd missed out on growing up. Or at least, he hated that it was a bronze or copper spoon he grew up with rather than a silver Birmingham one."

"That is a possibility." He turned to Emma Jane again. "Care to weigh in here or just wait for your attorney?"

We were met with silence again.

I shared the last bit of my theory. "I think she showed up at the marina to meet him, probably figured it was a safe place since Lester could be bribed. Jonathan loved to push buttons, though." I looked at the stoic woman sitting across from me. "He was really good at getting under people's skin. I can almost understand why you would snap and take the kayak paddle to him. I don't even believe you went there with the intention to kill him."

There was one more detail I really wanted to understand. "Why frame me, though? Admittedly, I've pushed a few buttons of my own with your family over the past couple days. Also, I know you were upset about me getting the storefront, but pinning a murder on me is extreme, don't you think?"

At my admission, Jeremy cut me a look. "What buttons did you push?"

I shrugged. "I can share details later. The point is I sometimes use that method to get people to open up. It's a gift." I ended my admission with a smile, but Jeremy didn't appear impressed.

Emma Jane let out an evil laugh. "Oh, the framing was just poetic justice. You march into town with all your pretty baubles and trinkets and think everyone should just bow down to the mighty Sadie Sabatini. When I saw you used the same paddle I did, it was just too good to pass up."

Without even meaning to, she'd pretty much offered up a confession to both me and Jeremy. Though she hadn't been read her rights and it probably wasn't admissible, I could at least share the details with the chief. Hearsay was better than nothing sometimes to cast doubt into the mind of the jury. "It was you who tried to break into my garage, wasn't it? You wanted to switch paddles so they'd find me with the murder weapon. Why didn't you just break the window or door to get in?" I'd figured the tests on my paddle had come back negative so the switch hadn't occurred, otherwise this day would have ended very differently for me.

Her head raised high, she donned the haughty expression I'd come to appreciate from her. "I am no common criminal. It's not like I knew how to pick a lock."

The irony of her statement made me laugh. She was anything but common, that was for sure. She wouldn't vandalize property, but had no issues killing a man. I'd let her therapist in prison sort that out for her.

My time to irritate Emma Jane ended as the police department arrived. Deputy Matthews moved to get me out of the boat. "I knew you were guilty. Doesn't take Sherlock Holmes to figure that out."

The pride in his expression and the way his chest ballooned with his statement made me more than pleased to watch both deflate. I turned to Jeremy. "You want to clarify the situation for him?"

Jeremy shook his head and shot me a disapproving glance, but there was a twinkle flashing in the golden flecks of the most beautiful eyes God had ever given a man. "Ms. Birmingham is the one you need to take into custody."

The air whooshed from Deputy Matthews' chest in a heartbeat, and he cast a worried glance from Jeremy to Chief Parker. "You can't be serious. We know it was her!" He pointed his knobby finger in my direction.

Jeremy didn't miss a beat, simply handing the kayak paddle over to Chief Parker. "I'm pretty sure this will have the evidence you need to make your case. Ms. Sabatini was the victim here. I'm sure she'll want to add attempted homicide and attempted breaking and entering to whatever charges you and the district attorney decide to levy against Ms. Birmingham."

I might've been falling in love with this man. It didn't matter that I couldn't. I shouldn't. Or that he wouldn't return that sentiment. The heart did things for reasons that defied reality all the time. Okay, maybe it was too soon for love, but it didn't change the pitter patter of my heart when he was around and went all Southern gentleman on me.

Chief Parker slipped on a pair of gloves and took the murder weapon from Jeremy. I couldn't help but add, "I assume you'll be returning *my* paddle to me first thing in the morning."

The chief smiled but shook his head. "Once our investigation is complete, all evidence will be returned." Yeah, this man liked to push all my buttons, too. I had to respect that about him, even if it annoyed me. What was good for the goose and all…

Deputy Matthews still looked like a deer caught in the headlights as he helped Emma Jane out of the boat. He was being very gentlemanly, and I couldn't resist asking, "Shouldn't you be cuffing the suspect, Deputy? I'm pretty sure that's proper protocol, and I know how important that is to you."

Yeah, I was being petty, but I didn't care. She'd made my attempt at a new life extra hard just because she had dropped the ball on the property she wanted. Then, she tried to frame me for murder. She deserved a little pettiness.

Jake shot a look at his boss, who gave a slight nod of his head. He was a by-the-book kind of guy through and through, so he knew it had to be done. "This is crazy. I'm sorry, Ms. Birmingham." Deputy Matthews slipped the cuffs onto her dainty wrists.

The irony of the situation didn't escape me. By all accounts, he should have been apologizing to me for wrongly accusing me time and time again. But I decided to let it go. See how much I'd grown just in the past week or so? I did hate that my phone was somewhere where I couldn't snap a quick picture of Emma Jane in cuffs. Oh well, maybe I'd need to attend her trial to get the money shot.

Jeremy's hand on my elbow brought me out of my musings. "You ready to get off the boat?" He smiled a bit, probably knowing where my thoughts had been headed. Okay, most likely not. He was a stand-up guy, after all.

"Sure." I took his hand, allowing for the boost up to my property.

Once I was on dry land again, Chief Parker stepped in

to ruin any moment I might have with Jeremy before he had to go back on patrol. "I'll need you to come down to the station and make a statement."

I sighed. "Can I at least change into some dry clothes first?"

Only if the game warden here agrees to escort you after you've changed. I don't want you skipping town and hurting my case."

I cast a hopeful glance at Jeremy. "You okay with that?"

He looked at his watch. "I only have about thirty minutes left in my shift, so that shouldn't be a problem. I'll radio in to let them know what's happening."

Chief Parker nodded and then helped Deputy Matthew escort the now cuffed Emma Jane to the waiting squad car. I noticed a few neighbors were now out on their back decks checking out what all the commotion was about. Sure, *now* they were curious.

Jeremy finished the call into his office to let them know what was going on. While he did that, I retrieved my phone. I had three missed calls from my father, two from Kelsey, and one from EZ. It was going to be a long night I sent a quick text to my father thanking him again for his help and letting him know I was okay. I promised to call tomorrow, and I reassured him it wasn't going to be a collect call from the county jail. He responded with a "whew" emoji. At least, that's what I thought it was. My father and emojis weren't on a first name basis. I also sent a quick text to Kelsey letting her know we'd catch up tomorrow. EZ, however, I called.

She answered on the first ring. "What in blazes is going on?"

"How do you know anything is going on?" I was truly

curious. It wasn't like I thought anyone who witnessed all of this was BFFs with EZ.

"One of your neighbors noticed Emma Jane being led away in cuffs. They called Robert."

Ah yes, the grapevine was strong in Wilson. "I'm sure he'll be arranging the finest of attorneys to try to get her out of this murder wrap. How's JJ?"

"He's sobering up. I'm not sure there's enough therapy hours available to help this family now." I could hear the sadness in her voice. She really cared about the Birminghams. Well, Robert, anyway.

"If there's one thing I've learned about the wealthy, they're resilient. Listen, can I catch up with you soon? They need me to make a statement."

"Yeah, sure. Just wanted to make sure you were okay."

Ah, she cared about me. That was sweet. Maybe we would form some kind of friendship, after all. "Thanks, EZ. What are you going to do next?" Between all the money, property, and blackmail material she'd inherited, the possibilities were endless for her.

"Keep working, keep living where I'm living, and use the money to help the people who need it most. I liked my life just fine before all this, and I see no reason to change it."

Oh, if only everyone had found the peace and contentment in their life that EZ had. "Sounds good. And the blackmail material?"

She sighed. "If it's criminal, I'm turning it over to the chief. I want no part of it. If it's petty, I'll return the evidence to the proper people and move on from the ugliness."

"You're good people, Estelle. I don't care what anyone else says or thinks."

She chuckled. "You're not so bad yourself, Sadie. Let's catch up later this week."

"Sounds good."

When I hung up the phone, Jeremy was standing there looking at me with a smile. "Look at you making friends."

I smiled, thankful he was counted among those I considered a friend. My thoughts took a negative turn as I thought about my kayak paddle. He noticed what must have been a worried look on my face. "What's wrong?"

"I was just thinking about my paddle."

"I know Chief Parker. He'll return it to you as soon as possible. I promise. Until then, do you have another one you can use?"

I nodded. "Yes, yes. That's not what I'm concerned about."

"Then what?"

"Her paddle has been in the lake probably several times since she used it to kill Jonathan. Plus, I'm sure she cleaned it. Do you think they'll find the evidence necessary to convict her?" The thought had me worried. While I didn't think Emma Jane set out to kill Jonathan that night, she definitely needed some professional help to deal with all the ramifications of her actions. And even though she hadn't intended to kill him, at the end of the day, she did. She now had a debt to pay to society and, ironically, to the Birmingham family for killing one of their own...even if they didn't realize it at the time.

Jeremy's warm hands rested on my shoulders, making me look up at him. "Hey, don't worry. Forensic science has a way of finding things that common cleaning products can't hide. They'll find what they need."

And I believed him, even if he was just saying it all to make me feel better. Though, he wasn't the type of man who would lie to a woman, even if he thought it was what she wanted to hear. I would rest easy knowing the wheels of justice would do their job...without my intervention this time. My days of that were over. I hoped so, anyway. I put my hands on top of his and squeezed gently. "Thank you for everything."

He smiled and released me, moving to stand beside me as we both looked out at the lake. "Just doing my job."

I bumped my shoulder to his. "Even though I was doing just fine on my own."

He laughed. "Of course, you were. Next time, I'll just wait and let you handle it."

The statement brought a huge smile to my face for the first time all evening. "Now *that*, sir, will get your gentleman card taken away."

He put his arm around me, pulling me tight against him. The warmth I felt would stay for many nights to come. "No, ma'am. We can't have that, so if you find yourself in trouble again..."

I slipped my arm around his waist and enjoyed the closeness for as long as he would allow. "You'll be my first call."

No further words needed to be said as we both watched the moon slowly appearing in the night sky over the beautiful Lake Amore. Yes, life was good and my new life was off to an exciting and interesting start here in the beautiful town of Wilson, Texas.

Epilogue

The following Friday, I sat at a large picnic table surrounded by my new friends. Hank was grilling steaks that had set my mouth to watering and made my craving for red meat strong. EZ and Hank's wife were finishing up the side dishes inside Hank's RV. Kelsey poured wine and was fussing with Pete about whether it should be red or white. Pete was arguing it should be beer or whiskey. Tessa was arranging her sugary-filled offerings on a platter, and Emerson and Isabella were skipping rocks off the dock.

Life was good.

Once we all had plates and had enjoyed several bites, Hank started the conversation. "So, EZ, or should I call you Estelle now?" he teased, earning him a glare from her. "What's the latest gossip from the other side of the tracks?"

Apparently, that's how they referred to Wilson proper in their little community. EZ laughed. "Same as always."

Emerson jumped in. "Is Mr. JJ going to stay in town for a while now?"

Leave it to the kid to bring up the questions no one else would find the courage to ask. EZ smiled at him. "Yes, I believe he is. He's working on restoring the relationship with his family. They had...*have* a lot of talking to do."

"How did he find out about Jonathan?" That was a question that had me lying awake for a night or two. Had Jonathan told him the truth, or had he learned about him some other way?

"Actually, Ted told him. After Jonathan approached him with his blackmail attempt, Ted set him straight on the relationship he'd had with his mother. Jonathan made him prove it with DNA. The results came back showing a familial match. They put the dots together, based on what they both knew, and came up with JJ."

"Why didn't Ted tell Emma Jane all of this?" If he'd only shared the truth with her, maybe all of this could have been avoided.

EZ chuckled. "Because Ted remembered the nightmare he had to live through when he was dating Emma Jane and she thought he cheated on her. No way was he going to bring that subject up again. Instead, he reached out to JJ to ask him to come home so he could share information with him. He didn't want to tell him over the phone."

"Wow," was all I could say. "So, did Jonathan and JJ get to meet before his untimely demise?"

EZ nodded. "Yes, earlier in the day. He showed JJ the DNA test results, but JJ wanted to be sure, so he said he would submit his DNA to see if it came back as a match. Then, he promised to prove to the family that Jonathan was his and they would make up for lost time. He would make every effort to restore both of them to the Birmingham name and legacy."

Emerson piped up before I could ask the next question. "Then, why did he meet with Ms. Emma Jane? Why would she kill him?"

Isabella shot Emerson a disapproving glance, but since I think she wanted to know as well, she said nothing to retract the question. EZ looked at him with sympathy. "Because sometimes, my boy, greed makes people do things that have serious consequences. Murderous consequences in this case. He must have figured until the DNA tests came in, he could get more money from Emma Jane's family. Maybe it was to make them pay for denying him and his mother the life he thought they would've had if Lydia hadn't left." She frowned. "But we'll never know for sure."

Kelsey joined in. "Yes, and those consequences can cost you everything. The Birminghams have already launched a public relations campaign to distance themselves from the McIntyre family and Emma Jane. Poor Ted is beside himself."

EZ shrugged. "The elite are protecting themselves, and the Bizzys are still trying to get rid of our home. Though," she smiled, "with her biggest ally fighting for her life in the justice system, I'm thinking there won't be much fuss anytime soon. At least, not until Karen finds another partner in crime."

"That's sad and so wrong," Emerson commented.

Isabella offered a half-hug as she put her arm around him. "Sometimes, life is sad and people aren't good. That's why rays of sunshine like you are so important."

I raised my glass. "To rays of sunshine."

Everyone else joined in with a "Here, here!" while Emerson blushed furiously.

Hank raised his glass...red wine, of course. "Well, all of that may be going on over on that side of the tracks, but here in our little slice of paradise, the finest regular folks in Wilson are enjoying some of the best Nolan Ryan steaks money can buy as the sun starts to set over Lake Amore."

As I raised my glass to support his toast, my phone buzzed with a text. I glanced down and saw it was from Jeremy. Three words that made my heart go pitter patter. *Dinner tomorrow night?*

He'd finally managed to ask me to dinner first.

I smiled and lifted my glass higher. "Fabulous food, friends, and a fine sunset. Life doesn't get any better than this. Thank you, my friends, for welcoming this newcomer into your fold and showing me how wonderful life in a small town can truly be. Here's to living our best life, no matter what obstacles may come our way."

The clinking of glasses and the voices of my new friends echoing the sentiment about living their best lives made me believe that maybe, just maybe, I'd found my forever home.

Acknowledgments

Special thanks to my critique partner, Vanessa Knight, for sharing your valuable feedback with me not only for this story, but since the very beginning!

To Harbor Lane Books and their wonderful staff – I appreciate all your assistance in helping me share Sadie's story.

Last, but certainly not least, to all my wonderful readers who have been with me from the beginning. Thank you for the love and support you've shown over the years and for the joy you've brought to my life by allowing me to share my stories with you!

About the Author

USA Today Best-Selling author Nicole Leiren likes to have fun -- in life, with her characters and, of course, family and friends. A Midwesterner at heart, she now proudly calls South Texas her home and lives with her husband on a beautiful peninsula in Lake Conroe.

Nicole enjoys sharing the laughter, mystery, and occasionally a little mayhem she forces her characters to endure all for the reader's pleasure! Her stories allow you to take a break and immerse yourself in a page turning story until you reach the whodunit or happily ever after (usually both!)

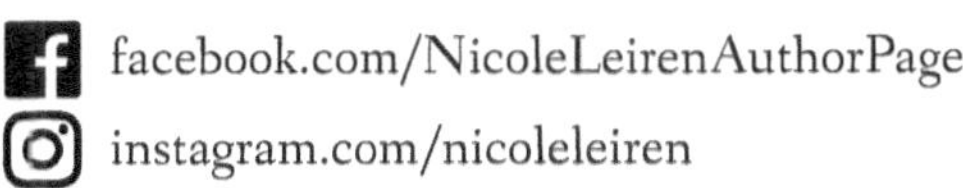

facebook.com/NicoleLeirenAuthorPage

instagram.com/nicoleleiren

About the Publisher

Harbor Lane Books, LLC is a US-based independent digital publisher of commercial fiction, non-fiction, and poetry.

Connect with Harbor Lane Books on their website www. harborlanebooks.com and on social media @harbor-lanebooks.

facebook.com/harborlanebooks

x.com/harborlanebooks

instagram.com/harborlanebooks

tiktok.com/@harborlanebooks

threads.net/harborlanebooks

pinterest.com/harborlanebooks